THE ALTAR OF VENUS

THE ALTAR OF VENUS

BY ANONYMOUS

CARROLL & GRAF PUBLISHERS, INC.

New York

Carroll & Graf Publishers, Inc.
260 Fifth Avenue
New York, N.Y. 10001

ISBN: 0-88184-001-7

Printed in the United States of America

Introduction

Despite the fact that this story is the erotic autobiography of one of our most famous contemporaries, whose name is known to only the secretary of this society, it is replete with action and thrills. It goes far beyond the usual run of erotic literature. It is a man's frank and honest search of his soul for the answer to that world old question: The riddle of the universe—Why and How is SEX and to what depths does it go. There is nothing to compare to it outside that field of psycho-sexual case books.

A word here as to how this manuscript fell into our hands. Without being too explicit we can say that sometime during the past two years there passed away one of the leading members of British Society. A sportsman, a Member of the House of Lords, one of the pillars of our National church, he was never known as a libertine. His memoirs have now shown him to be also a Prince in the peerage of Pornagraphia. In his declining years he apparently achieved sexual satisfaction thru his reminiscences. He, no doubt, little dreamed that they would some day be put before other eyes.

When his estate was being settled his secretary had opened the wall safe in his home and this manuscript was discovered. Fearing that the publication of such a revealing volume would blacken his late employers reputation he ordered the butler to burn it in the furnace. This latter worthy gentleman upon repairing to the basement to carry out the order chanced to glance at a couple of pages and, while astounded, realized that such a treatise could mean money to him. He secreted it and at the first opportunity came to the undersigned. After perusing page after page, since I could barely put it down, I knew that here was a real find. I am quite sure that our members will appreciate that the price we paid for it was but small in comparison to its value.

The reader will find it scientifically accurate to the last detail. It is most illuminating in its portrayal of the love-life of one who thought of woman as the first consideration in life. No other work, within our knowledge so faithfully exposes the varied erotic urges that beset mankind.

Chapter I

Children! Are they the same the world over —does sexual precocity break out amongst them in certain localities at certain periods, something like an epidemic of measles from which few are immune, while in other places and at other times, they escape unscathed? Certain it is that my own childhood was lived in an atmosphere redolent with sexuality and this despite the fact that my home environment was of the best. My parents, indeed, held to the most Puritanical notions and doubtless would have been literally dumbfounded with horror had they ever gotten the slightest hint as to what was taking place almost under their very noses.

Either their own lives had matured under conditions quite different from mine or the passing years had obliterated all rememberance of juvenile delilitry for assuredly no suspecion as to what was transpiring about them, almost, as I have suggested, close enough to be smelled, ever arose to preoccupy their well-ordered lives during my childhood days.

Confidences exchanged in later years with adult friends indicate that while many went thru experiences similar to mine, the lives of others were singularly barren of juvenile romance or precocity. To the lips of the former, therefore, my stories may bring a smile as old memories are stirred, and they are carried back over the highway of years by the narration of some incident which had a counterpart in their own lives, and to the latter, a sigh of regret at something missed in life.

I do not propose to fill up space with the narration of incidents other than those which some curious, unique or laughable element justifies their telling. With this brief prelude, I begin my story.

I was born in the year 1900. My birthplace, an English city, with some thirty thousand population. My parents, though not rich, were moderately well off and we lived in the comfortable fashion of the middle class English family. I was an only child and as such was humored to a certain extent, but I was also ruled with disciplinarian firmness, for my father, a grave, silent man, was quick enough to take note of juvenile insubordination, and as quick to chastise it. I held him in great respect, with which was mingled a certain degree of awe.

I place the age at which I experienced my first sexual excitation definitely identified with a female at somewhere between five and six. I say definitely identified with a female because even prior to this I had observed a periodic hardening and expansion of that curious little appendage that hung between my legs, which phenomena generally occurred in the early morning, or when I was being bathed. More than once I had been on the point of asking my mother for an explanation of its peculiar conduct, but some instinctive reticence always sealed my lips just as the question was mentally formulated. Certainly, up until almost my eighth year I was entirely unaware of the difference between the sexes and blissfully ignorant of all things pertaining thereto. But about the time I was six years old the association of a female was for the first time linked up with erotic sensations. It was of a rather insignificant nature and transpired under the following circumstances: For a year or more my mother, failing in health, had been confined to her room. There was in the domestic employ, an elderly woman who acted in the capacity of general housekeeper, and amongst whose varied, and multiple obligations devolved that of watching over and endeavoring to keep me out of mischief. When I was about six years old, she retired from our service and in her place came a maid of seventeen or eighteen. Her appearance was attractive, her manner genial, and I soon developed a strong liking for her.

This girl had been duly authorized to punish me for disobedience, or other infractions of the household peace, corporal punishment being the prescribed remedy. But she was a good natured, kind hearted damsel and it wasn't until I had committed a particularly malevolent piece of mischief one day that she lost her temper momentarily, turned me across her knee, and gave me a paddling. The blows were not of sufficient severity to cause me any real discomfort, and something about the position in which she held me across her knees, or perhaps some dormant instinct awakened by the contact of her hand on my bottom, began to work on my sexual nerve centers and resulted in a muscular reaction similar to that which I had observed on other occasions already referred to. In addition, I now became aware of a decidedly pleasurable sensation which was stealing through my body, a sensation which seemed to be forming in and radiating from the regions about my groins. The condition I was in must have become apparent to her through the pressure of a hard little cock against her thigh for she abruptly discontinued the chastisement, and I perceived a smile on her lips as she stood me back on the floor.

From that time on I sought ways and means

of securing repetitions of this pleasant punishment, and the obliging damsel, entering into the spirit of things, accommodated me generously. But the method first employed was improved upon. Subsequent spankings were not administered, without first lowering or removing my trousers, and while the spanking was in progress the amiable girl held me in such a position that while one hand was dealing blows of just enough vim to warm my naked bottom, the other could be insinuated under my groins, and cupped over my cock and testicles. The soft pressure and contact of her hand upon these organs caused me such exquisite tremors as to motivate constant efforts on my part to provide her with pretexts, which I instinctively sensed to be necessary, for more and better spankings.

Now, it might reasonably have been expected that these little incursions into the realms of concupiscence would have paved the way to others of a more advanced nature. But such was not the case; she never ventured to extend the simple repertoire, nor did it ever occur to me to so much as wonder what she might have between her own legs. For upward of a year the spankings continued and then, much to my regret, she took her departure from our midst. And though it concerned me not the slightest at the time, I often speculated in after years as to precisely what there had been for her in all this and what pleasure she could have derived from the performance. Possibly the mere handling and fingering of my small but eminently masculine attributes in their state of sexual ex_ citation reacted upon her own sensibilities, provoking a species of reciprocal echo. At any rate, I remember her with the kindliest feelings of appreciation.

I was seven years old when I made an important discovery. In the yard which surrounded our home were a number of trees. Among them was one of the eucalyptus variety, slim and straight as an arrow. Some six or seven inches in diameter at the base, its verdant bark as smooth as silk and not a branch or twig to mar its lissom symmetry for thirty or forty feet above the ground. There was something distinctly feminine about this young tree. Perhaps it was the smooth, beautiful bark, and its slender gracefulness which set it apart in vivid contrast with its gnarled and rugged companions.

One afternoon, having nothing better to do, I endeavored to climb this tree by the "shinning" process. As you may not know just what the term means I will explain that, having no limbs or protuberances within reach which would provide foot holds, the only way to climb such a tree was to wrap one's arms and legs tightly about the trunk, and by virtue of much wriggling and squirming, work one's way upward inch by inch. I had succeeded in hunching myself upward a short distance in this fashion when I began to feel again that delicious tremor which the hand of our erstwhile maid had formerly provoked. It was being produced by the friction and rubbing of my cock against the tree. When I realized this I clamped my legs tighter and wriggled more energetically and the more I wriggled, the more pronounced became that teasingly, pleasant sensation. I redoubled my efforts, and abruptly something seemed to burst down there inside, and as it burst, a wave of delicious sensations was radiated through my body from head to foot. I had experienced my first orgasm. Half dazed, forgetting that I was at some elevation, I relaxed my grip on the tree, and half slid, half fell to the ground, where for some moments I lay in a state of amazed wonder. When my wits returned, I essayed another climb, but the nice feeling refused to repeat itself. Another effort the next day was more successful and needless to state, that tree was for some time hence the object of my most fervent adoration. So I may say with all truthfulness that my first sweetheart was a slender young tree. I remained faithful to this love until in the due course of time, I found that the nice feeling could be reproduced in a far simpler and much less arduous manner namely, a little manual manipulation, and then the tree went into the discard.

At nine I was in my second year of school and was being initiated (in theory) in the mechanism of love by well informed young companions. An intriguing word of four letters was being constantly brought to my attention as it appeared mysteriously chalked on the walls of toilets, sometimes in more public places. The little girls snickered, giggled, or blushed at covertly whispered words, or signs and motions. Or with simulated indignation threatened to "tell the teacher." I knew now that these little girls had something between their legs entirely different from what boys had; something in the nature of an opening, provided for the express purpose of having a boy's cock inserted therein, and that when so inserted both parties to the transaction enjoyed ineffable delights. And my heart hungered for practical demonstrations. But, alas, I was not of a bold and forward disposition, and could not bolster up my courage to the point of asking a girl to "do it" with me, the proper formula, according to my more venturesome comrades. And so, I had to content myself with listening to their tales of conquests, while my heart was consumed with envy. I would have blushed with shame to have been obliged to confess it, but up to this period I had never so much as glimpsed in a single instance that mysterious region between a little girl's legs. True, they played and disported themselves at times with careless abandon, in which short dresses were well elevated, but they invariably had on panties which effectually concealed the salient point of interest. With what enthusiasm would I have hailed a law probiting the use of panties by girls.

There was one for whom I eventually came to feel an overwhelming passion, but my love was mixed with awe, I guarded it a close secret, nor ventured by word or act to convey any indication of its existence to the object of my adoration. Her name was Flora. A golden haired little fairy who wore her hair in long curls. Flora's age was about that of my own or possibly a little younger. I watched and admired from the distance, and was filled with rage when one boy, a coarse, displeasing fellow in my opinion, calmly observed that he had "done it" with Flora. It was a lie, I felt certain, a bit of bragging designed to awaken the envy of his hearers, but I hated him cordially from that moment and on the slightest provocation would have picked a fight with him.

I passed my waking hours in day dreams of

Flora. Before falling to sleep at night I imagined delicious situations in which she and I were thrown together under circumstances which forced us to sleep together. We were marooned on tropical islands, or lost in the wilds. In fancy I hugged her naked body to mine, touched and caressed her limbs, fondled her to my heart's content and delighted my eyes with the vision of her nude loveliness, to fall asleep at last with my cock sticking straight up while Flora danced through fantastic dreams.

'Tis said that all things come to him who waits. And one Saturday afternoon I passed by a vacant lot in which a group of youngsters from my neighborhood were playing. Flora was amongst them. Somebody shouted my name, calling me to join them. Not having business elsewhere of sufficient importance to offset the pleasure of being near Flora I immediately accepted the invitation. Little did I suspect it at the moment, but wonderful things were in store for me that sunny June afternoon. It is thus that Fortune favors us when we least expect her grace.

After a while the charming little mistress of my heart approached me, and with a friendly smile on her face, whispered:

"Let's you and I run off and play by ourselves."

Had the sun suddenly turned green I could

not have been more surprised. It was the first time she had ever addressed me except in the most impersonal manner. Furthermore, the secretive way in which she had communicated the little message, the furtive look she cast toward the others as she whispered it, were pregnant with romance. My heart leaped with pleasure as I nodded my conformity.

"All right! Come on!" she answered in a low voice, and together we slipped away unobserved by the rest. When we had rounded a corner, and were out of their range of vision, she again placed her lips close to my ear and shielding her mouth with her hand, whispered:

"Let's go to the park and play married!"

The surprise I had received when she first addressed me was nothing compared to the electrical effect of this second communication for the expression "playing married" had a very concise, and unmistakable meaning in our little world—a meaning which admitted of no misinterpretations.

The part she referred to was an extension of land which traveresed the northern section of the city and which was destined some day to become a public park, having been purchased by the municipality for this purpose. At this time however, it was nothing but an uncultivated tract of ground, overgrown with weeds and wild shrubbery. Through the center of this terrain ran a deep gulch in which water had sometime flowed. It was dry now and there were occasional deposits of clean, white sand in the boulder strewn bed. Its precipitate banks were overhung with vines and wild vegetation.

This so-called park enjoyed a peculiar reputation among the young folks. It was referred to with sly looks and smiles for it was supposed to be the scene of most of the amorous adventures which took place between juvenile gallants and accommodating misses. Certainly, the secluded nooks and refuges available amidst its verdant shrubbery lent themselves admirably to the game of "playing married."

So off we trotted and five minutes later, breathless and flushed, we were at the outskirts of the park described. We slipped under a wire fence, and were soon scurrying through the underbrush toward the gulch itself. When we reached it we followed its bank until we found a place which afforded a safe descent, and then, jumping, slipping and sliding we reached the bottom.

From the beginning Flora had taken the initiative. I accepted her leadership, and acquiesced to each suggestion she offered. I was still tongue-tied with timidity. Truly, the female of the species is, at certain ages, more venturesome than the male! After a short exploration we found a cozy little nook almost entirely concealed behind a curtain of green foliage, an ideal little love nest requiring no alterations except the clearing away from its sandy floor of an accumulation of rubbish and dead leaves. We set to work and quickly cleaned out this refuse until nothing remained but clean sand. Satisfied with the results of our labors, we sat down to rest for a moment. The position in which Flora was sitting afforded a generous glimpse of her tight little panties and between this and other anticipated revelations my nerves were tingling with excitement. After a short silence, during which she eyed me expectantly, she suddenly arose and exclaimed:

"Well, if we're going to play married, you have to take your pants off! I'll take mine off!"

And suiting action to word, with perfect sangfroid and without the least embarrassment she raised her dress and unfastened the garment to which she had referred. It slid down her legs and was kicked off to one side. I got up and began fumbling with my own buttons. My fingers were numb and torpid and it was an interminable length of time before I got my trousers and underwear off. And now I became aware of an embarrassing condition which further contributed to my confusion. One which on two or three subsequent occasions in my life made itself apparent much to my mortification an disgust.

Something which on countless occasions ha risen valiantly at the mere thought of seein Flora naked and which had been standing u manfully while we were arranging the nest, no failed me treacherously and was hanging wit its head down in the most listless and dejecte attitude possible to imagine. Flora gazed at i a moment and exclaimed:

"Why, your dickie isn't stiff yet!"

There was no denying this allegation, and remained silent. However, she evidently regard ed the condition as amenable to correction, an with worldly wisdom, added:

"Look at me between the legs and it will ge stiff!"

So saying, she lifted her dress and separatin her thighs, arched her body outward so that he little cleft was exposed in all its juvenile nudity

What were my emotions, as I stared wide eye at that tiny portion of feminine anatomy which had so long intrigued my imagination, and o which I was now gazing for the first time in actu ality? Too mixed and confused to render a des cription possible. My fascinated eyes perceive that what I had supposed to be something in th nature of a hole or a round opening was instea a narrow cleft—a cleft resembling a tiny valle between two plump little hills. A valley that, starting from a little dimple, coursed downward, and curved inward between her thighs. It was like the letter "V" with a straight line down through the center! Surely a boy's thing couldn't be pushed very far into that tight, narrow little place. Probably it was only supposed to be rubbed along the length of the little valley, between the fat little hills.

Meanwhile the efficacy of Flora's homeopathic remedy for impotency was making itself apparent, and my cock began to straighten out. It lifted itself upward with little jerks, and before many moments it was standing out horizontally, as firm and hard as it had been before.

As soon as she was satisfied that its condition was favorable to her purpose, a condition she verified by extending her hand and testing its rigidity with her fingers, she twisted her dress around her waist, and lay down on the sand. I knew enough to place myself on my knees between her open legs. Inclining my body forward over hers, I managed to get the head of my cock between the plump little lips and commenced to bob up and down, pressing and rubbing against her.

She stood this curious treatment for a few moments and then pushing me from her, she sat up.

"Silly! That isn't the way! You have to make it go in!"

Without waiting for apologies, she extended her body out again on the sand, took my cock between her fingers, got the tip of it inserted and started in the right direction, and with a sudden upward heave secured its complete intromission. Guided by instinct I raised and lowered my hips in unison with the undulating movements she imparted to her own. The friction of her hot little genitals and their moist embrace as they clung to, and sucked at my cock brought the natural reaction, and as the preliminary tremors of ecstasy began to make themselves felt, I accelerated my movements. And with the acceleration the pleasure intensified. Frantically I worked my cock in and out of the tight, wet little lips which clung on it so caressingly.

Ah, if I could live them over again I would draw those happy moments into hours of delight, extending and prolonging each precious, celestial second into indefinite lengths. But alas I knew nothing of the principles of conserving energy or scientific methods of prolonging to its utmost the all too fleeting pleasure and thought only to reach the culminating, divine instant as quickly as possible.

Just as I was trembling on the verge of a

sterile but deliciously sweet orgasm, her legs flashed up and engaged themselves tightly about my body, and from her lips emerged a series of exclamations which testified to the measure of her own sensations. She clung to me for a moment and then her arms relaxed their grip about my neck. She disengaged her legs from my body and lay back upon the sand. There was an expression on her face, as she eyed me covertly from under half closed lids, which denoted something of surprise as well as satisfaction.

We got up a few minutes later and I took a final look at the little bisected "V" at the base of her stomach which had provided me with what would probably be the tenderest memory of my life. In silence she replaced her panties, smoothed out her clothes and stood waiting for me to finish dressing. Then, when we were ready to leave, she snuggled her hand into mine, glanced shyly at me and murmured:

"Gee, it felt nice, didn't it?"

That night as I lay awake reviewing the momentous event I suddenly remembered that despite all the castles in air I had built up in my imagination around just such an occasion, I had not kissed her when the opportunity was at hand. No, not a single kiss or caress of any nature aside from the copulation itself. Nor had I scarcely more than touched with my fingers

that seductice and mysterious little cleft. An
part of my complacency changed to chagrin a
I realized all I had missed by my silly bashful
ness.

From that day on my character began to un
dergo a change. My shyness and reticence fel
away and while at certain times it returned t
plague me temporarily, I was generally bold and
venturesome whenever I had the slightest reason
to think I knew my ground.

My next rendezvous with Flora was effected
through my own initiative. Our relative positions
changed and it was I who assumed the leader
ship. Her manner toward me was respectful
submissive, as if in a certain sense she belonged
to me, and this time I put into execution every
fancy my inexperienced mind could conceive.
petted, caressed, fondled and handled her to my
heart's content. I made a close ocular examina
tion of the mysterious domain between her
plump, white little thighs. I even ventured t
explore the interior depths with an inquisitive
finger. To all this manipulation she submitted
patiently, apparently gratified at my interest
When I had looked, handled and caressed my
fill, I placed myself between her outstretched
thighs, and without any false movements this
time, got my cock into her, and handled it to

such good effect that we were both soon gasping with pleasure.

After this I progressed rapidly. Not to be outdone by other boys who boasted of many conquests I began to make advances to other little girls, and was amazed at the facility with which I obtained their complaisance. Some indeed repulsed me—there were girls like that—foolish little things, who wouldn't know what was good for them—but there were plenty of others, and so I mentally consigned the obstinate ones to the dark regions, and devoted my attentions to those who were amenable to reason. Flora herself presented a little friend who blushingly confessed to a desire to "try it" once. To my mystification, an intact hymen in this instance obstructed a successful demonstration and in my ignorance of feminine physiology I attributed the failure to a sad defect in her little body— she had been born without a hole! I had yet to learn that maidenheads were at a premium.

A boy friend confided that he had "done it" with his sister, aged twelve.

"We were playing up in the hay loft in the barn and I got her down and looked at her cunny. Then she wanted to look at mine, and so I let her. Then I told her she had to do it with me. She didn't want to, but I made her. Now we sneak up there and do it lots!"

The girl in question was such a sedate quiet Miss that I was much astonished and really doubted the truth of the story, but it aroused my lubricity and I asked him if he would get her to do it with me too. He said he would, and his efforts as an "ambassador" of love in my behalf were so successful that an agreement was promptly arrived at. Upon an altar of sweetly scented hay, under the dusty rafters of the old barn, the blushing, but willing victim of this libidinous sacrifice to Venus was offered up. Sans panties, and with dresses up she permitted me to take my place between her outstretched legs and drain the cup of love while her young brother looked on complacently. When I had finished he quickly took my place, and without undue embarrassment at my presence, inserted his small cigar shaped cock in her and gave her a second work out.

The next day she communicated to me by means of a note surreptitiously slipped into my hand at recess that if I would wait for her after school at a certain place we could "do that again that we did yesterday."

Another little youngster of nine or ten, a veritable Mesalina in the budding, conceded her favors to four of us "en masse". In the basement of the deserted schoolhouse, to which we gained access through an unlatched window one Satur-

day afternoon, she stripped off both panties and
dress for our edification, and one by one, un-
troubled by an excess of spectators or hygienic
considerations we took turns in prodding her
with our small, but rigid little cocks.

According to orthodox theories these little
girls were all on the road to inevitable ruin if
not already there. Yet to my personal knowledge with respect to several of them, they grew
up, married and lived normal and respectable
lives. One indeed who had been particularly
liberal with her favors—I doubt if there was a
boy in the entire neighborhood for whom she
hadn't removed her panties at least once—I met
some sixteen years later. At first I failed to rec-
ognize in the modest, well dressed young matron
and mother of a beautiful child of two, a former
youthful partner in fornication. But something
stirred in my memory and without stopping to
think that perhaps she would prefer not to have
the past recalled, I asked her if she hadn't lived
in such and such a neighborhood in her childhood. She nodded assent. "Don't you remember
me?" I asked impulsively, repeating my first
name. "No, I don't recall you!" she replied.
"Why, I—" and then I saw that her cheeks were
blazing. Belatedly, my own face burning with
the sudden comprehension of my tactless interrogation, I changed the subject.

At thirteen I was growing rapidly, was quite tall and well developed, this also contrary to certain other accepted theories for according to all authorities on the subject, such excesses as I was indulging in should irrevocably have undermined my health. For in addition to fucking every little girl I could wheedle into removing her panties I also masturbated myself with more or less frequency. One day I ran across an old medical book containing drawings and diagrams of the human form in various stages of revelation. The book intrigued my purient interest, and while searching it for more illustrations I came upon a chapter on masturbation which, hastily read, chilled the blood in my veins and sent me flying to a mirror to see how many of the visible signs, so luridly described, were visible in my own countenance. According to this book, boys who practised the destructive vice were recognizable under a cursory examination. Their eyes were dull and lifeless, the lids discolored and swollen. Their faces were sallow, and even their self-conscious and nervous demeanor was sufficient to betray their guilty secret. All unfortunate boys addicted to this vicious habit were doomed. Insanity, consumption, premature old age were all lurking close at their elbows. A rapid calculation as I rushed to a mirror told me that I had been at it for four years or more, and it was indeed with a sigh of relief that I scrutinized the reflection which gazed back into my anxious eyes. No signs of senile decay were visible. My complexion was clear and rosy, my eyes bright and limpid. And I certainly was not undersized, for my physique was such that I was generally taken to be at least two years older than I really was. A prolonged examination dissipated my fright, but I had received a shock, and thereafter I indulged in masturbation only on special occasions. As the book said nothing about anything disagreeable happening to boys who fucked little girls, I assumed that no evil consequences need be anticipated from this direction.

At fourteen, I was associating with boys several years older than myself, some of whom had had experiences with adult females, some even with prostitutes. In the light of their revelations, my own little adventures seemed insipid and infantile. I learned of mysterious houses where one could go and have his choice from among a number of luscious young females on display in the nude. There was a certain section of the city allotted to their special occupancy, whole blocks of buildings devoted to the traffic of commercialized sexual pleasures.

Grown women! It must feel much nicer to do it with an adult woman than with an immature, inexperienced little girl! The thought grew, obcessed me, set my fancy on fire. And still I dared not think of trying to enter one of these palaces of delight, for though I knew where they were located, boys under eighteen were not supposed to be admitted. I could pass for sixteen easy enough, but hardly eighteen.

One of my friends became the envied owner of a packet of pictures of nude women. They were passed from hand to hand. I persuaded the fortunate owner to let me take them home with me over night. I wanted to enjoy them in private, at leisure, in the seclusion of my room. One by one I examined them with my cock sticking up and threatening to go off by mere force of mental stimulation. What took my eye was the fascinating triangle of curly hair which stood out so prominently on the pubic regions of the models. None of the little girls I had had dealings with had hair down there, or at least more than a soft, incipient, almost imperceptible growth. The thick, curly profusion which adorned the sexual regions of the ladies in these pictures held my eyes in fascination. What an exquisite sensation those crisp curls woult provoke as they tickled one's cock and testicles! And their breasts, full, round and luscious, projecting outward like snowy hills! Not a girl I knew had anything to compare with what these pictures revealed.

As I studied them, my hand unconsciously dropped downward over an erected cock which was fairly bristling with fury. And, unable to resist the urge, I jacked myself off with rapid strokes. As orgasm took place several jets of milky fluid sppurted outward. My testicles were secreting semen and I now constituted a first class risk to damsels of twelve and upward who were indiscreet enough to let me squirt that hot starchy looking stuff between their legs. When the last drop had been squeezed out, I sighed, hid the pictures under my mattress, and turned out the light.

I wanted a mature woman, one who had hair around her cunt and big breasts and I wanted her with all the ardor of my being. But there was no woman I dared approach. Then, as unexpectedly as golden haired little Flora had entered my life, Fortune led me, or I might say, actually shoved me, right into circumstances which culminated in the fulfilment of my ambition.

Among my acquaintances was a boy by the name of Gerald. Having interests in common we formed a species of alliance although he was somewhat younger than I. He invited me to his home and thus I came to meet his mother. One look and I was head over heels in love. She was everything imaginable in feminine pulchritude.

Around thirty but still conserving a youthful beauty which might well have been the envy of women much younger, small and petit of figure, a pair of bubbies which projected her blouse out in front in the most amazing manner, she fairly made my mouth water. I could hardly take my eyes off of her during the time I was in the house. She was a widow, Gerald's father having died years previously. Evidently she had married at a very tender age. It was apparent that Gerald was the pride of her life, and any of Gerald's friends were treated with royal consideration. My visits became frequent, and I was invariably regaled with cake, mince pie, plum pudding or other gastric delicacy. But it wasn't the cake, or the pie, or the pudding which drew me. I came to look, and long, and sigh. Presumably my passion was unsuspected, but at times she seemed to be eyeing me with a quizzical, understanding expression on her face.

One afternoon Gerald and I decided to entertain ourselves by making and flying a pair of kites. We secured paper, twine, sticks, and other essentials. While engaged in this for once entirely innocent occupation, Gerald's mother brought us two big glasses of lemonade, and some chocolate cake. She was going to town, she said, and was serving us this luncheon so we wouldn't get hungry meanwhile.

Gerald and I finished our kites, and carried them to the square six blocks distant. He soon had his floating in the sky, but mine, solicitously guided by the finger of Destiny, tried to argue the right of way with an electric light wire and before I could extricate it was badly damaged. Repairs necessitated both paper and paste, so while Gerald remained, I returned with the intention of getting these essentials from his mother. When I reached the house I ascended the front steps, and rang the bell. There was no response. As I waited, I suddenly remembered that she had, presumably, gone to town. In a tentative way, I tried the door and found somewhat to my surprise that it was unlocked. Knowing exactly where to find the things I desired, I opened the door and walked in. From the parlor a hall led to the kitchen and in this direction I turned my steps. I was exactly half way thru this long hall, when the door to the bath room, just ahead of me, swung open and Gerald's mother stepped out into the hall, fresh from the tub and strip, stark naked except for her hose and slippers.

It would have been difficult to say which of us was the most astounded. We both froze in our tracks gazing at each other wordless with surprise. I opened my mouth to make some explanation, but a correct formula of apology to offer a

lady under such circumstances was beyond me
and I closed it again without having uttered a
word. There seemed to be a haze in the air
which partially obscured my sight through it I
perceived a black triangle which gradually resolved into a glossy silky profusion of tight little ringlets of hair, sharply outlined against a
background of snowy whiteness. As this became
fixed on my consciousness, something down in
the front of my trousers began to hoist itsef upward. A low, strained voice broke the spell:

"Where is Gerald?"

Mechanically the answer fell from my lips.

"He's down at Wellington Square with his
kite."

The expansion in the front of my trousers had
reached its maximum, causing a tent shaped projection outward. I was still gazing thru a sort of
cloud, but it seemed to me that she was smiling
faintly. The next thing I knew she was standing
close in front of me, and had placed one of her
hands on my shoulder. The other slipped down
inside the waist band of my trousers. A bit of
fumbling with underclothing and soft cool fingers closed around my cock. They remained
there for a moment and were withdrawn. I felt
them tugging at the buttons in the front of my
pants.

One, two, three, four little tugs, and like a

jack-in-the-box released at the touch of a spring, my cock jumped out into the light of day as the clothing which had imprisoned it was loosened. Again soft fingers encircled it and with a forward movement of her hand the scarlet plum shaped head was exposed to view. The hand receded and it disappeared from view within its protecting shield. The movements were repeated a few times, sending little electric thrills chasing up and down my spine. And then a soft voice murmured in my ear:

"You've been hanging around here with this thing sticking up under your pants to tempt me for the last three months. Can you keep a secret?

I nodded my head affirmatively.

"Well then run and slide the bolt on the front door before someone else comes walking in!"

My heart was pounding with excitement as I ran to obey. When I returned, she opened the door to her bedroom, and motioned for me to enter.

"Take off your clothes!"

I was still flushed with emotion, but I was recovering my composure, and as I stripped off my clothing, my eyes were devouring the delectable spectacle of her nudity. Pretty as she was dressed, she was a hundred times prettier naked. How different she looked from those flat chested little girls with their small bottoms, their bodies, except in one single detail, little different from those of boys! Her full round hips, her narrow waist, her maturely symmetrical legs and thighs, her breasts so big and white, with their luscious carmine nipples. Even as I looked, those luscious strawberry-like tips seemed to be changing in form. They were puffing out, taking on a deeper hue, projecting themselves forward seductively.

And, charm of charms, that fascinating profusion of dark ringlets of hair which formed as true and perfect a triangle at the base of her stomach as though drawn by rule and pen. Plainly visible under the inverted point of the triangle, could be seen the clean-cut incision of her sex as it curved gracefully inward between white, round thighs. Observing my trembling excitation and wide-eyed wonder, she broke into laughter, and throwing her arms about me began to kiss me, exclaiming:

"Haven't you ever seen a woman naked before, darling?"

"Yes...I...that is...girls...." I answered, my voice trailing off in confusion.

"Girls?" she prompted, "What girls?"

"Why...ah...lots of them, girls in school!"

"School girls?" she repeated, in surprise, "What do you mean, darling? Girls don't take off their clothes at school, do they?"

"No, no! After school I mean, in the park,

"You surely don't mean they take off their clothes in places where boys can see them naked, do you?"

"Yes, m'am."

"Girls how old?"

This interrogation was making me uneasy, still I sensed the fact that I was safe in confiding in her. "Oh, all ages," I answered, rather vaguely. "I did it with one girl that's past 12."

"You did it! Are you trying to tell me that you've really had intercourse with some of those little girls?"

"Sure, I have!" I answered disdainfully. "Lots and lots of them!"

"But darling," she gasped, "I can't believe it! Little school girls are not even supposed to know about such things! Why, good heavens, you couldn't make this go in a little girl without hurting her!"

"It doesn't hurt all of them!" I insisted, stub_bornly. Which was true enough, for I hadn't in fact encountered many maidenheads.

"Well, it doesn't seem possible," she comment-ed. Suspending for the moment the interroga-tion she led me to the bed, lay down upon it, and drew me over on top of her.

Soft fingers took possession of my cock, and guided it quickly to the entrance of the humid recess between her thighs. Now she placed her hands over the cheeks of my bottom. A firm pressure, a gentle movement of hips and thighs and the turgid emblem of my sex was within the portals and I felt the contact of thick, crisp hair against my flesh. She undulated her hips with a gyratory movement and almost immediately that "nice feeling" began to generate itself around the principal point of contact and was radiated thence in delicious little waves thruout my body. I raised and lowered my hips in unison with her own movements.

All too quickly the humid warmth and suction vanquished my limited powers of resistance, and soon the spermatic liquid was being drawn from my testicles. As I moaned with pleasure the pressure of her hands on my bottom became more forceful and her movements more energetic She gasped some unintelligible phrase, a convulsive shudder shook her body and...it was all over. I lay quietly with my weight upon her body until my heart ceased its excessive beating. Then raising myself, withdrew my dripping cock from between her thighs. She gave it one look and springing hastily from the bed, exclaimed:

"My heavens! You're old enough to give me a baby, if I don't watch out!"

She ran into the bathroom and after a brief absence returned with a damp towel, with which

she sponged me off. Assuming that my hour of
triumph was over, I reached for my clothing but
she detained me with a gesture and suggested
that I lie down and rest a few minutes first. So
willingly enough, I lay back down on the bed
again. She lay down by me, slipped an arm under my neck and drew my face over against one
of her protruding, pointed breasts. I pressed my
cheek gratefully against the cool, smooth flesh.

"Now tell me about those girls," she insinuated, softly.   And bit by bit she drew from me
the gist of my juvenile romances. These disclos-
ures seemed to cause her the most genuine surprise. While we talked one of her hands en_
gaged itself with my cock. She slipped the foreskin back and forth, fingered and toyed with it.
Between this tantalizing manipulation, the sight
of her naked body, and the erotic effects of our
conversation as she pressed me for intimate details of my conquests, it began to recover its dig-
nity, extending itself perceptibly in length and
breadth.

"Do all the boys in school do such things?"
she asked, her fingers continuing their soft play
over the head of my cock.

"Sure; they all do," I answered, innocently.

"Then Gerald has been doing it , with girls,
too?"

"Gerald? Well....I don't know about him!"

I answered in confusion. She remained silent and recovering my composure I ventured to extend my tongue, and rather timidly caressed one of those luscious, red strawberries which was in tempting proximity to my lips. I felt a tremor pass over her body and encouraged, I took the whole strawberry in my mouth and sucked it avidly. Immediately her fingers tightened around my cock and she began to pump it vigorously. I became still more daring, and placed my hand down over the triangle of dark curls. And, after a momentary hesitation, I laid my finger on the warm, moist membranes of her cleft.

In the course of my education in sexual physiology, I had learned that in the upper extremity of the little valley, just like a sentinel on guard over the sacred precincts, was a little protuberance which had a predilection for being petted gently. It had the odd faculty of enlarging itself slightly when touched or caressed, its reaction in this respect being similar to that of the male organ.

Putting this knowledge into effect I located the highly sensitive little nerve, and with the tip of my finger agitated it softly. Under the light touch it responded by expanding and hardening. At this point she suddenly seized my hand, and laughing hysterically, removed it. She kissed me with real fervor and pressed her body closer to mine.

"Come on sweetheart, we'll do it once more!" Disengaging herself from my arms she turned over on her back, and separating her thighs, drew me up upon her. Again my cock, now well restored to virile capabilities, was introduced into the tempel of love. The encounter was swift and vigorous. I seconded her lively movements, and again those hot lips drained my testicles to the last drop. Shortly thereafter I was dressed, and ready to take my departure. As I stood near the door, she kissed me good-by, adding in an anxious whisper: "You won't ever, ever tell anyone, will you, sweetheart?" Fervently assuring her that I never, never would, I took my leave.

At the front gate I met Gerald, who greeted me angrily.

"Where have you been all this time?" Did you get the paste?"

"Paste? I repeated, vaguely, "Paste?" Why ...ah, no, there wasn't any!" And leaving him staring at me open-mouthed, I continued on up the street. Kite flying no longer interested me.

With the optimism of youth, I assumed that the romance so auspiciously begun, would be continued. But alas, I was doomed to disappointment. Whether the lady repented of her little indiscretion, or decided that I was too young to be trusted I know not, but at any rate, never by word or sign did she encourage me to expect a repitition of the adventure, and eventually I comprehended that the chapter was closed.

During the year which followed I made a number of conquests among young girls of the neighborhood but do not recall of any which were of special interest. It was not so easy now as it had been at first. Girls had to be won with courting, coaxing and artifice. They protested hypocritically at bold advances. They were afraid they would "get a baby." And how it happened that none actually did only heaven knows, for some of these young misses were close around the age of puberty, as was attested to by the fine growth of silky hair on their little mounts, and diminutive, budding breasts.

I found that successful dealings with them hinged mostly on coaxing them into some secluded place where there was no danger of intrusion or interruption. Once this was accomplished, a preliminary kissing and petting to get them "hot" followed up by the sudden insertion of a hand up under their skirts and panties was generally sufficient to get things started. There would be a few squeals and protests, but the tip of a skilled finger played over and around a certain magic little spot generally vanquished the half-hearted resistance. The system was simplicity itself, but almost invariably successful.

One thirteen-year-old, who claimed to have learned the method by spying on her parents when she was supposed to be sleeping, permitted me to penetrate her but to my surprise, just as I reached orgasm, jerked away from me and seizing my cock with her hand, pumped its contents out over her naked stomach. This proceeding she denominated by the expressive term "milking the cow", adding that it caused her a nice feeling when the warm stuff squirted out on her stomach.

With greater frequency now my thoughts were on those intriguingly mysterious houses so picturesquely described by older companions, where charming young ladies were at one's disposition for a modest consideration.

But it wasn't until I had passed my sixteenth birthday that I got up courage to make the plunge. A sudden wave of boldness inspired the determination, and in order not to give it a chance to cool off, I decided to act immediately.

That night, nerves tingling with anticipation and excitement, I set out on foot for the red light district. Approaching an establishment selected entirely at random, I stepped inside and closed the door behind me. I paused for a brief moment and then mustering up my courage, advanced toward an open door. Enveloped in an azure haze of smoke I saw a nearly furnished room in which were seated or moving about, a dozen girls and several men. The girls were in varying stages of dress and undress. Some were garbed in chemise, high heeled slippers and hose only. Others had on diminutive silken skirts which hung about halfway to their knees. One or two were draped in vividly colored kimonas. Another, crossing the room at that moment with a tray of liquor glasses in her hands—an attractive damsel with a mass of copper colored tresses, and a skin as fair as a lily, was stark naked except for hose and slippers. Her beautiful and prominent breasts vibrated and trembled with her movements.

Quickly my eyes took in the scene, impressing upon my mind a composite picture of silk clad limbs, naked thighs, breasts, arms, and a not displeasing array of faces. The girls were young, much younger than I had supposed they would be. As I stood motionless in the door taking in the novel sight, a sudden hush fell upon the assembly, and all eyes were turned on me. There was a momentary silence. Then a feminine voice exclaimed: "The stork has brought a baby for someone!"

A burst of laughter followed this cynicism and my cheeks began to burn. Then from among a group of girls seated on a sofa one arose, and came toward me, smiling: "Do you want a girl to take to a room?" she insinuated coaxingly.

I knew that patrons were supposed to select their own merchandise, but my nervousness and the embarrassment their risibility had provoked inspired me with a desire to get out of the range of all these curious eyes just as quickly as possible and I assented to her invitation with a nod of my head. She took my hand and conducted me down the long hall to her room. Once the door closed behind us and we were in privacy, some of my animation returned and I examined my companion with deep interest. She was a wholesome, sweet faced girl of eighteen or nineteen and her cordial, friendly treatment quickly put me at ease. The financial details of the transaction arranged, she stripped off her little, silken chemise and while I was removing my own clothing, occupied herself with the preparation of a basin of warm water to which she added soap and a few drops of some fluid, probably of an antiseptic nature. As soon as I had disrobed she approached me and holding the basin, washed my cock in the soapy water. Under the touch of her soft fingers as she manipulated it in the warm fluid, it stiffened out valiantly.

As she bent over, her hair falling in glossy ringlets about white shoulders, her pretty cone-shaped breasts vibrating with each movement a sense of satisfaction and exhilaration swept over me and I placed my arms around her neck, drew her face up and kissed her with enthusiasm, almost causing her to drop the basin. Hastily she set it down and proceeded to dry me with a small towel. Then, after pirouetting about the room for a few moments to tantalize me with the sight of her nakedness, she flung herself on the wide comfortable bed and invited me to follow her.

I was soon lying between her round white thighs while her fingers started my cock in the right direction. Then in and out, with slow deliberate movements at first and faster and faster as the pleasant sensations increased in intensity, and finally, with hard furious thrusts as she drew from me the milky elixir of life. As it spurted forth, she clasped me more closely to her and gave expression to several passionate exclamations. I didn't know at the time that simulating orgasm is an art quickly acquired by these little vestals of love whose business it is to always "please" the customer.

After she had attended to certain hygienic requirements, she returned to the bed where we lay for a while exchanging confidences. Her name was Josephine. She assured me, greatly to my satisfaction, that I was much nicer (!) than most of the men who visited her, and extracted a promise that I would come back to see her, a promise which was whole-heartedly and became real friends with Josephine.

Some of the other girls attempted to win me from Josephine but on observing that our relationship was firmly cemented they desisted. As a matter of fact, there were several I would have liked to "try out" but a spirit of loyalty to Josephine who was so good to me and the fear of hurting her feelings kept me faithful. Her affection for me was evidently quite sincere and she counseled me wisely in many things.

During the petting and teasing processes which generally preceded our expansions I discovered that she was partial to digital manipulations, or in brothel terms, finger frigging. This condition was probably due to some abnormality, or possibly the too frequent copulations in a profes_sional capacity had dulled the normal reaction. At any rate her emotions could not be completely, aroused any other way and I think the fact that I was able to perceive this condition, and was considerate of it, inspired to some degree the affection she felt for me.

While gratifying her in this way I learned to subject and hold my own emotions in check for prolonged periods and this is an asset which cannot be too highly estimated. Not only does it sharpen the sensory nerves, making them more responsive to the delayed orgasm but it also places one in a very advantageous position with respect to women. The pleasurable sensations which accompany ejaculation in the male are far more intense with the first orgasm than with a second or third. Apparently, the "pleasure capacity" of the masculine sexual organism is depleted or dulled greatly by the first ejaculation and does not respond with the same vigor to successive efforts unless there is considerable time between.

The unnatural life led by girls in houses of prostitution, submiting their bodies to sexual intercourse without regard to their personal inclinations, frequently with men abhorent to them tends to stultify and deaden their sensibilities. Josephine had not reached this stage. She was only two years older than I and as yet showed no signs of dissipation. Her clear, grey eyes and rosy cheeks sparkled with health, life and vim. But she didn't like the way the men "did it"— on top, finished and off before it hardly began to feel good. She never really enjoyed herself except with me, she said!

One day when I came in I noticed some of the girls running in and out of the parlor, laughing and giggling about something the nature of which I was in ignorance. When Josephine and I were alone I questioned her as to the cause of the merriment. "Oh, it's that Swede who comes to see Marigold," she replied.

The man she referred to was, like myself, an afternoon visitor. I had seen him on several occasions sitting in the reception hall, waiting for Marigold, the object apparently of his undivided affections. He was a quiet, polite fellow, large of stature, always plainly but neatly dressed. How they had come to designate him as "the Swede" I don't know unless it was that his blond hair and Nordic accent someway suggested the nationality. As Josephine replied to my query, she too began to giggle and my curiosity was further aroused. "Well, what's so funny about it?" I insisted and as I spoke, there flashed over me the recollection of previous instances when, after the departure of this man I had observed smiling glances directed at Marigold—Marigold, the girl I had seen cross the room naked the memorable night of my initiation in sporting life— who was also blond and whose copper colored tresses, and big breasts had always secretly fascinated me.

At first Josephine seemed disinclined to enter into explanations, but her reticence only augmented my curiosity and I persisted with the result that the following novel facts came to light.

This man, despite his robust appearance, suffered from a lamentable physical defect. His cock was less than half normal size, and incapable of attaining an erection of sufficient rigidity to penetrate a woman. The only way he could satisfy his passion was by sucking a girl and jacking himself off at the same time. For the privilege of sucking Marigold once a week he paid a generous fee. But this wasn't all of the story. These little devils had scratched away a bit of paint from one corner of a glass transom above a door connecting with Marigold's room and were in the habit of entertaining themselves by watching while the sucking operation was being realized. "Does Marigold know that?" I asked, astounded.

"Sure, she knows it. She doesn't care," replied Josephine, but he doesn't." Instinctively I cast an apprehensive glance around our own room, to see whether there were any "scratched transoms" through which I had possibly been subjected to the scrutiny of curious eyes. Josephine read my thoughts and said smiling, "Don't worry, we don't do anything worth watching!"

Her revelations turned my thoughts to subjects I had hitherto not given much attention to. I had heard of "frenching" of course, but regarded the act as being of rare and unusual occurrence. Yet here it was going on right at my elbow and seeming to excite nothing but amusement among those who were aware of it. Josephine noted my absorption, and asked curiously:

"Do you want to look?"

I hesitated but a moment, and replied affirmatively: "Come on, then."

She slid off my knees and led me to a room further down the hall. With her finger on her lips in a gesture signifying silence she opened a door, and we edged in. To one side was another door and before this, perched on a table which had been drawn up before it, were a couple of half naked girls, each trying to peer through a glass transom from one corner of which a bit of paint had been scraped away. Josephine pinched their legs and motioned to them to get down.

"He's just begun!" whispered one of them as they slipped down, albeit reluctantly, their faces suffused with suppressed laughter.

Josephine and I took the places they had yielded. She applied her eye to the small opening for a second then clutching my arm, she withdrew to one side, permitting me to look. I looked, and held spellbound by a sight which caused the blood to race through my veins.

On the opposite side of the room into which I was peering and not more than eight feet distant was a bed, and lying across this bed, entirely naked, except for her hose and high heeled little slippers, was Marigold. She lay with half her body extended across the bed, her legs down over the side, her feet resting on floor. Kneeling between them with his mouth pressed to her cunt was the Swede. One of his hands was under her bottom and the other was busily engaged in tuning up his undersized and half erected cock. It appeared to be about the size of that of a child of eight or nine. Marigold was laughing hysterically and at intervals her legs flew up as though actuated by springs released by the man's tongue. He was going after it with all the vim and relish of a hungry youngster tackling a piece of custard pie. As he progressed, the movement of his hand on his own diminutive member became more rapid. From time to time Marigold glanced covertly upward toward the transom quite aware apparently, of the fact that unseen spectators on the other side were enjoying the unique exhibition.

I ceded my post of observation to Josephine. She watched a moment and her hand closed over mine.

"Quick! They're finishing!" she whispered sibilantly, and moved to one side. Again I applied my eye and was just in time to see the conclusion of the spectacle. Marigold was not laughing now. There was a strained, set expression on her face seemed to be trying to effect a closer contact. now clasped about the fellow's head and she and in her wide staring eyes.

The Swede's hand was moving so rapidly the eye could scarcely follow it. A convulsive shudder passed over Marigold's body. She released his head from her grasp and sank back on the bed. As she did so, she put one of her feet against his shoulder and violently pushed him away from her. He fell over backward on the floor, his undersized cock rapidly lost its slight erection, and curled limply down on his stomach. The show was over.

I climbed down from the table, lifted Josephine down, and without a word we repaired quickly to her room. I was in a veritable frenzy of lust and had hardly gotten my cock into her before the semen was flowing.

The result of this episode was to set me thinking along new lines and I questioned Josephine rather extensively about "frenching" as the lingual, or bocal stimulation of the sexual organs is vulgarly called. There were establishments known as "french houses" where this particular kind of service was specialized in almost exclusively.

I revolved the subject over in my mind. Here was a new tid-bit on which to speculate. The idea intrigued, and at the same time repelled me. The feminine genital organs had never seemed to me as being of an unclean or repulsive nature. To the contrary, I had always experienced a keen pleasure in touching, fondling and caressing them. But the idea of placing my mouth where other men had placed their cocks was highly distasteful to me! Had it not been for this detail I would have looked on the practise with relish.

Josephine would have submitted to me, if for no other reason than to enable me to satisfy my curiosity but I could not overlook the fact that she was daily in contact with other men, and this dampened my enthusiasm. As to being "frenched" myself by one of these girls that was a different matter. And the more I thought of it, the more clearly was I able to imagine the delightful sensations which would accrue thru having one's spermatic fluid sucked out by a woman's warm mouth. And I made up my mind that at some no distant date I was going to visit one of those naughty "french" houses.

My relations with Josepphine had been of nearly a year's duration, when one evening at the dinner table my father announced his intention of spending a few weeks with his brother in the country. While discussing the projected vacation, he casually remarked that, were it not for interrupting my schooling he would have con_ sidered taking me with him. Ordinarily the prospect of any kind of a journey would have

my instant enthusiasm, but even as lips parted
to make the plea, it occurred to me that such a
trip would interfere with a certain project I had
in contemplation, namely, a visit to one of those
French houses, which I was even then saving up
money to finance. And so, hastily revising the
words I had been on the point of uttering, I murmured something to the effect that it would indeed be inconvenient to absent myself from my
school at this particular time. This indiscreet
remark attracted my father's attention. He
looked at me speculatively for a moment, and
said: "Yes, I believe I'll take you along with
me. You've been studying too hard lately. I believe you need a rest, too."

There was an inflexion in his tones and an
understanding in those steely blue eyes which
caused me to lower my head, and I interposed
no further objections to accompanying him.

My uncle went in for scientific farming, was
quite prosperous and had a fine home in which
were to be found all the modern comforts, and
conveniences possible in a rural community. A
week after the conversation above referred to
had transpired found us on the night train, and
early the next day we reached the small station
where a carriage drawn by two powerful horses
was waiting to convey us to the farm a few kil-

ometers distant. And shortly thereafter we were at our destination.

I was in no humor to greatly appreciate the beauties of nature in full bloom, but as I glanced around and observed the stately elms, the well kept gardens, beautiful vines and flowers which surrounded a long rambling, comfortable house, with green fields, and azure tinted hills in the distance, my spirits rose somewhat, and I consoled myself with the reflection that even here the necessary ingredients of an amorous adventure of some kind might be found. For my uncle's farm provided a livelihood for several families, which lived on the premises in little houses and cottages and which almost constituted in themselves a small community.

One afternoon, tired of reading, I was discontentedly wandering to and fro among the various barns and granaries on the place when I suddenly and unexpectedly came face to face with a young person of whose presence on the farm I had not previously been aware. This young person was a pretty rustic damsel of thirteen or fourteen. Recovering quickly from my momentary surprise, I bowed gracefully, wishing her a pleasant afternoon. She responded civilly, edged past me, and went on about her business—whatever it was.

Discreet inquiry revealed the fact that she was

the daughter of a widow woman who had charge of the butter and cheese making department, and that the two of them lived in one of the tiny cottages nearby. Immediately the situation took on a rosier hue and with great optimism I began to speculate on the possibilities. It will be gathered from this that I was lacking neither in self assurance nor vanity. My experience with girls had been such as to support the idea that my attentions not only were welcome but expected. Consequently, it was with considerable surprise I found that this country damsel did not respond immediately to my advances. Indeed, her attitude bordered on the disdainful. Though I managed to meet her at frequent intervals, adopting my most polished airs in my efforts to engage her in amiable conversation, she regarded me in the most expressionless way, briefly answering such questions as I propounded in futile attempts to hold her attention—and proceeded on her way. This was for me a new experience. It exasperated me, and incidentally, shocked my sense of the fitness of things, that this calico gowned, bare legged country girl was not impressed by my city airs and sophistication. However, aside from being pretty, she possessed a pair of bubbies of dimensions truly amazing in a female of her years, whose contours, blooming floridly and visibly under the scant clothing, fairly mesmerized me. So I redoubled my efforts. But, alas, my most persistent and assiduous attentions failed to envoke a spark of interest, and finally, I abandoned the siege in disgust.

Again I took recourse to the library as a means of diversion, and it was while rummaging through the well stocked shelves that I encountered a book with a French title which attracted my attention. I withdrew it from among its companions and idly thumbed the pages. They were uncut, but the chapter titles in the index fed my interest. I took the volume out to my hammock and with a penknife cut the pages. The title of this book was "Madamoiselle de Mauphin." How it happened to be in the library of my puritanical and religious minded uncle I will never know but it was certainly due to some accident and beyond doubt he never so much as suspected the presence of this masterpiece of lurid literature in his staid and respectable collection of books.

I had not, up to this time, ever gotten my hands on any book of a really pornographic nature. The family doctor book, with its chapters on procreation, childbirth, and kindred subjects was a far throw from the book I at that moment had before my eyes. Many times since I have tried to obtain a copy in English, but such as I have found invariably turned out to be re-

vised or "expurgated" editions. In the certainty
it would never have been missed, I could have
appropriated this copy if I had had my wits
about me at the time. The story revolves around
a young French girl who, thrown upon her own
resources adopts a masculine disguise as a protection against the vicissitudes of life to which
an unprotected girl would be exposed. She is involved in many erotic situations, which culminate
in another young girl falling in love with her,
unaware of her true sex. This girl, frantic at her
apparent failure to win du Maupin's love enters
her room at night and in a last despairing effort to seduce the object of her infatuation, exposes her nude body. This, and many other emotional episodes, in the last of which the two females come to a satisfactory understanding, surrendering themselves to each other in a sexual
embrace of mysterious nature, were so vivid in
their rendition that I was soon in a state of erotic frenzy. Before I had concluded many chapters I arose from the hammock, sought the seclusion of my room, and lay down on the bed
to continue the story. Soon I was obliged to unfasten the front of my trousers for comfort.
Shortly thereafter I was holding the book in one
hand, and masturbating myself with the other.
The necessity of being at the dinner table interrupted me before I had finished the story, and

tucking the book under the mattress of the bed, I went downstairs. Later, pleading a headache as an excuse for early retirement, I returned to my room. Before I turned out the light that night I had read the book from cover to cover. And incidentally had jacked myself off three times.

This orgy of masturbation, instead of calming my nerves seemed to have just the contrary effect, and throwing discretion to the winds, I resolved to force an issue with the dairy woman's daughter. I had dealt with girls before whose real, or simulated objections to intimate relations had been vanquished by bold and forceful methods and, though this girl's attitude toward me was rather at variance with anything previously experienced, I decided to adopt a course involving more action and less talk with her. Maybe that was what the sly little minx was waiting for.

Through more or less clandestine observation, I had learned something of her habits and knew that at about four o'clock each afternoon she made the round of the barns and stables to gather up eggs which the hens, allowed to run at large, deposited in obscure nooks and corners. In one of the stables there was a loft in which a reserve supply of loose hay was stored. I had seen her going up the stairs to this loft and it was in this ideally situated and "furnished" retreat I planned to waylay her.

And so, pulses beating in optimistic anticipation of carnal intimacies with her, I waited the opportune moment and when she entered the building that afternoon I was close at her heels. As I reached the door she was ascending the narrow stairway, and I slipped quietly up behind her. On reaching the top of the landing I saw her in the other extremity of the loft gathering up eggs from a nest in the side of a pile of hay. As I approached her she glanced at me but there was no expression of alarm in her face. She continued to pick up eggs which she placed carefully in a basket. Falling back on the old tried out and proven system, I wasted no words this time in idle conversation. Putting my arm around her waist, I sat down on the fragrant hay, and pulled her down upon my lap. She uttered not a single word, nor made the slightest movement of resistance, but simply laid passively in my arms. I pressed my lips to hers, and though she did not return the caress, neither did she try to avoid it.

I had expected something in the way of a mild resistance at least, but things were going smoother than I had anticipated. Delighted at the facility with which the long deferred conquest was being realized, and lulled into a false sense of security by her seeming complacency, I relaxed my grip on her, and without further preambulations put one of my hands up under her dress and inside the loose panties she had on.

Barely had I sensed the contact of silky hair and the moist flesh of her cunt against my fingers when, galvanized into action, the little wild cat sprang from my lap and dealt me a slap on the side of my head so terrific that my ears buzzed for an hour after. And, before I could recover my wits and get to my feet, she was off like a flash, and flying downstairs.

This misadventure brought disagreeable consequences. The candid girl told my aunt that I had done something "nasty" to her. From my aunt the accusation was transmitted to my uncle and thence to my father, bringing down on my shamed head such a lecture as I never before had been obliged to listen to. Lying like a trooper, I denied the allegations, maintaining that I had done nothing except kiss her under tempting provocation. But she was called in for a more specific explanation as to just what it was "nasty" that I had done to her. And to my exceeding motification, she convincingly maintained that I had put my finger in "that place" between her legs. Specific enough! I was in disgrace for the rest of our stay. When the visit came to an end, and we were on the eve of departure, I heaved a thankful sigh of relief. As far as I was concerned, the vacation had been, with the exception of a few pleasant hours spent in the company of Mademoiselle de Mauphin, a complete, and perfect failure, and I could hardly wait to get back to the city and Josephine.

Chapter II

Six weeks of enforced continence, unbroken
except for the orgy of masturbation inspired by
Gautier's erotic story, had added fuel to the fires
of concupiescence which burned within me. My
relations with Josephine had been of nearly a
year's duration and throughout their course I had
enjoyed sexual gratification on an average of
once a week. It was in effect, almost as though
I had been married for this length of time and I
felt keenly the want of something she was in the
kindly habit of providing me. So, as I enjoyed an
imagination the love feast, which I knew would
be accorded me on my return, my cock stiffened
out in anticipation of the delights in store for it.
I adjusted my clothing, permitting it a more
comfortable position in its expansion and as I
did so an inspiration came over me which caused
my heart to beat faster, and my cock to get still
harder. Why not celebrate my return to the city
by carrying out that long deferred, but cherish-
ed project of paying a visit to one of those mysterious "french" establishments? What more fit-
ting occasion to appease my curiosity along this
line for once and all and at the same time exe-

cute a species of revenge on Fate, for the morti-
fying events recently transpired?

I would do it! We reached home at noon, and
I spent the rest of the day in preparation for the
adventure, scarcely able to restrain my impa-
tience for night to come.

Around nine o'clock that evening I slipped
out of the house unobserved and set out on foot
for the sporting district, and towards one of
these houses I directed my steps. Exteriorly, it
was no different in appearance from the many
other houses of protitution which lined the street
but I had been definitely informed that it was
a "french" house. Without permitting myself to
hesitate I opened the door and ascended a long
flight of steps which led to the upper floor.
Here I found further progress barred by a locked door, but an electric button, conspicuously located, suggested the correct procedure, and I
pressed it tentatively. A few moments later a
small panel in the door slid back. A short interval elapsed during which I was evidently under
the scrutiny of some person behind the door,
then it swung open and I found myself confronted by a buxom female who smiled expansively
at me and invited me to enter.

She led the way to a reception room and, as
on the occasion of my initial visit to the place
where Josephine was located, I found myself in

the presence of a number of females in varying stages of nudity. For some reason, probably the fact that it was a Monday night, there were few men present. My gaze swept over the assembly, and was returned expectantly by the females upon which it momentarily rested. Seemingly, several different nationalities were represented by the women present.

I edged into the room and seated myself in a chair near the door, glancing uncertainly from face to face in search of one which appealed to me. I was not overly sure of my ground. These girls did not appear greatly different from those where Josephine was, except that some of them were patently of foreign nationalities. In some vague, indefinite way I had expected women who did what these were reputed to do, to look different from others. I wondered uneasily whether maybe after all, I had been misinformed or had mistaken the address. As I glanced doubtfully from one to another of them, my eyes came to rest on a well proportioned dark complexioned damsel whose appearance was in some way suggestive of French nationality. Her plump thighs and legs stood out in seductive relief under the edge of a short pink camisole, so transparent that the profusion of jet black curls on her mons veneris was plainly visible. When she perceived that my attention was fixed on her, she came

over, seated herself confidently on my knee and
with her arm around my neck, murmured the
customary formula:

"Let's you and I go to a room, dearie!"

Time was precious, there was no reason for
delaying things and as I had already decided on
her in my mind, I accepted the invitation, and
she led me to her room. The dramatic moment
had arrived. Thrusting my hand in my pocket I
extracted all the money I had in my possession,
two pounds and a few shillings in excess. Surrendering the entire sum, I screwed up my courage and said in a low voice:

"Will you do it to me the "french" way?

"Sure, I'll 'french' you, dearie!"

The suspense was over. But while it lasted a
misfortune had overtaken me. Exactly as years
previously on the threshold of being initiated by
the golden haired little Flora, embarrassment
and nervousness vanquished virility at a critical
moment, and I now sensed the calamitous fact
that my cock was hanging down in inert and lifeless dejection. The perception of this disaster
brought a flush to my cheeks, and I would gladly have retired had I been able to think of some
pretext to excuse my flight.

The girl, unconscious of my embarrassment,
was already engaged in preliminary preparations, and was chatting away in an amible fash-

ion, but I was too engrossed with my own pre-occupations to hardly know what she was saying. Soon she was standing before me with a bowl of water in her hands and a towel over her arm, waiting for me to disrobe. There was no help for it and reluctantly I commenced to undress. She had removed her chemise, and was completely naked except for her little high heeled slippers and hose, but even the sight of her exquisitely rounded hips and legs, her protruding breasts, the rich profusion of hair that stood out so prominently at the union of her plump thighs were insufficient to revive the miserable append-age which hung its head so lifelessly between my own legs. And now, the last garment was off and its condition was revealed. Without evidencing any surprise, she took it between the fingers, and immersed it in the warm water, saying:

"You've never had it "french" before, have you, dearie?" I made no reply, and she continued:

"You're just nervous that's all. Lots of men are that way the first time. I'll make it stand up all right."

Meanwhile the girl kept up her amiable chatter to which I was now able to listen with more attention, and as my tranquiliy returned, I ventured to ask her a few questions. Her name was Rose. She was not as I had supposed,

French, but Belgian. No; she didn't like this kind of life. She was saving up her money to leave it and return to her native land. Some of the men who came were not nice. They were never satisfied, and expected a girl to do all kinds of things. Only last night, she confided, a man had wanted to do it to her in the bottom, and had gotten angry when she refused. Inwardly I marveled at the incongruous line of reasoning she must have employed to justify herself in taking a man's cock in her mouth, and at the same time maintain scruples against it in her bottom but I kept my thoughs on the subject to myself.

The abulutions now concluded to her satisfaction, she removed the basin, and inquired:

"How do you want it, dearie, single or double?"

Obvious as was the question I failed to comprehend it at the moment. Not wishing to display further signs of ignorance and as the world "single" sounded somewhat less formidable than "double" I replied with but a momentary resitation:

"Single."

What she wanted to know of course was whether I wished only to be sucked off, or in addition, also perform on her at the same time.

I started toward the bed, but she stopped me with a gesture, saying:

"Listen, dearie, I'm going to tell you something. You've never had it "french" before, and you're nervous. Don't lie down. Let me do it to you standing up. It will feel nicer that way."

Though surprised I acceded to her suggestion and under her guidance I leaned against the wall while she placed a cushion on the floor at my feet, and kneeled upon it.

The fifteen or twenty minutes which followed will remain engraved upon my mind as long as memory lasts. Fifteen or twenty minutes during which such waves of delight passed through my body, as set every nerve from the top of my head to the tips of my toes tingling with ecstasy, waves which alternately lifted me up on their crests to the heights of sublimest delight, and then gently dropped me back down to less turbulent but equally delicious realms of bliss.

On her knees before me, one hand clasping my testicles, the other resting lightly on my hips, she took my cock in her mouth. She began a slow backward and forward movement with her head with the result, that at one moment, only

the crown was between her lips, the next, half
its length was engulfed within her mouth. And
as the foreskin receded with the forward movement, exposing the head, she ran her tongue
around and over it and each time that hot tongue
passed over or curled around the delicate gland,
the sensation fairly stood me on tip-toes.

Had she wished to do so, she could have
brought this performance to its conclusion within less than sixty seconds, for I could not have
withstood the uninterrupted action of her tongue
and lips for a longer period, but she was evidently disposed to give me my money's worth
and with scientific exactitude she regulated her
lingual activities to coordinate them with my
powers of resistance, and each time, just as the
sensation reached its zenith of intensity she relaxed the tension just sufficiently to forestall the
impending explosion.

During the short interval this sybaritic ritual
was in progress I was a dozen times so close to
the crisis that through a feeling of embarrassment at the idea of ejaculating in her mouth,
I put my hand on her head to ease her away,
but she declined to release her grip on the pal-
pitating object between her lips and motioned
to me disapprovingly.

Finally, cognizant of the fact that the limit

of my endurance had been reached, she removed her lips and said:

"I'm going to let it come now! Don't move and don't try to jerk it away! Just stand perfectly still and let me do everything!"

She pushed the foreskin back with her fingers and took the exposed head between her lips. This time, there was no movement. Apparently she was just holding it in her mouth. But, ah! I felt a sudden suction alternated with curling and tapping of a soft tongue around the gland, which continued a few moments and then, suddenly the seminal fluid was spurting into her mouth. She continued the suction until the last drop had been withdrawn.

Rising quickly she spit out the spermatic libation and rinsed her mouth with several successive glasses of water. I threw myself upon the bed from which I watched her with half closed eyes.

And thus was my first experience in passive fellatio or, as it is vulgarly called in the language of the day, "being frenched" satisfactorily consumated, and I had enjoyed to the fullest that sexual caress which is probably the most exquisite of any known to mortals.

I have always, I fear, been afflicted with an excess of sentimentality, a defect which has caused me unhappiness and disagreeable complications on more than one occasion. In casual dealings with the fair sex, it is well to avoid sentimental weakness.

In plain words, a hot cock and cold heart make the best combination. When sentimental considerations begin to play too conspicuous a part in sexual affairs we are in for disappointment or trouble or maybe both. There is a funny superstitution prevalent among women of middle and lower class in England to the effect than a man will never forget a woman who has sucked his cock and young wives are frequently advised by older women to employ this unique method of firmly anchoring their husband's affections! As to what truth there may be in the allegation, I hardly dare venture to maintain but before twenty-four hours went by I wanted to see Rose again so badly, I could harly think of anything else. Financial considerations prevented my immediate return and was two weeks before I could accumulate the necessary funds.

I returned but when my eyes eagerly swept the assembly in search of Rose, she was not visible.

"Is Rose in?" I inquired, politely.

"No, she's gone." was the brief response.

"When will she be back?" I asked, my heart sinking with disappointment.

"She won't be back. She's gone away."

"Where can I find her?"

Nobody knew, or they did know which was more likely, they were not disposed to tell. Wouldn't another girl do just as well? Clearly, in the matter of having one's cock sucked, they were unable to see why any fine distinctions between girls should be drawn.

I shook my head negatively, my heart too full for words. I wanted Rose and nobody but Rose—the disappointment was too keen to consider a substitute. They all looked drab and unattractive in comparison with the vanished Belgian. I backed out of the door, went down the stairs I had ascended in such a pleasant glow of anticipation, to turn my steps disconsolately homeward.

A week later I paid a belated visit to Josephine. She received me with open arms, overjoyed at my return. Indeed so affectionate was her greeting that I felt a twinge of conscience for my dereliction and unfaithfulness.

There were few visitors in the reception parlor, and as it seemed probable that we would have the evening free from interruption we lost half an hour or more acquainting each other with what had happened in the interval of our separation.

Needless to say, I omitted to tell her about

Rose, and simply delayed my return to the city an extra two weeks to account for not having seen her earlier.

The story of my adventure in the country, which I confided to her quite frankly, convulsed her with laughter.

"What did you let her get away for?" she said, "when you start any thing like that you ought to finish it. If you had held her, and given her one good fucking she'd have kept quiet about it and been after you for some more pretty soon! Had her in a hay loft, and your fingers in her pussy, and then let her get away from you. I'm surprised!"

"I didn't exactly let her," I said and rather sheepishly explained how I had been defrauded by the slippery little country maid.

"Well, I won't try to get away, darling, but first, you know what I want! I haven't had a good frigging since you went away!"

She laid her head against my cheek, separated her legs, and I put my hand over her cleft. A few preliminary caresses, and my finger tips began to play with the little protuberance which was so responsive to their touch. She shivered with pleasure and murmured:

"Darn it, Gilbert, you could win a girl with just your finger even if you didn't have anything else. You've got just the right touch, and not one man in dozens ever learns it."

"Why do you like this better than the real way?" I asked.

"Oh, I don't know. Variety, I guess. I get it so much the other way it doesn't thrill me anymore. Maybe it's because I'm lazy. This way you do all the work and I just lie still and enjoy myself. Some like it better by hand than the regular way, too." she continued reflectively, "There was a girl here once, she left before you started coming here, that wouldn't do anything but frig men with her hand. She was awfully pretty, but everyone thought she was balmy to except to make any money that way. They called her Miss Jackoffsky in fun. But they soon found out she wasn't nearly as crazy as they thought. Men started coming and asking for her, and they kept on coming back, time after time, and the landlady finally decided she was frenching men instead of jacking them off. She fixed a hole in the wall of her room, and we watched when she had a man in the room. But there was no fake about it, she didn't do a single thing but jack them off with her hand. Sometimes the man would beg and coax her and offer her extra money to let him fuck but she never gave in and that same man would come back again in a few days. It was the strangest thing; she got so many calls some of the other

girls began to get jealous of her and were so
nasty to her she finally left. I bet you there
were men coming here asking for her for six
months after she had gone, and they never
would take another girl when we told them she
wasn't here. So you see, she concluded, smiling,
"I'm not any worse then some of you men. It
feels good, and I like it."

"A nice soft tongue would feel still better." I
ventured.

"It might, at that," she commented pensively,
after a moment's silence, "sometime . . ."

In this moment there came a sudden knock-
ing at the door, and from the other side, the
voice of the mistress of the establishment calling on Josephine to hurry, as there was a crowd
in the parlor, and all the girls were needed.

Inasmuch as I had already exceeded by far
the time I was entitled to occupy Josephine
there was nothing for me to do but disgustedly
put on my hat and coat and depart.

It was about eight-thirty and as I wandered
down the street, wondering how to most enjoy-
ably spend the evening with the small capital
in my possession, I saw a train with the sign
"Wonderland" approaching, and acting on the
impulse of the moment, I ran out and boarded
it.

Wonderland was an amusement park situated

on the outskirts of the city. Here were cheap
shows, skating rinks, carousels, and an infinity
of catch-penny devices. On holidays, Saturdays
and Sundays, the place was well patronized,
but there never was much activity on week
nights, although many of the concessions remained open. It was reputed to be a fine place
to "pick up" girls, although at this moment, I
had no other thought in mind than to kill an
hour or two of time agreeably.

When we reached the park I got off, paid
the small entrance fee; and went inside. Few
of the entertainment features were operating
but here and there were signs of activity with
barkers, pitchmen and touts shouting their wares
or extoling the qualities of the entertainments.
I idled along, indifferent to their supplications,
'for I had on previous occasions seen about all
there was to be seen.

From a distant section came the strident, but
not unmusical notes of a mechanical organ, operating in conjunction with a merry-go-round, and
towards the source of this music I wended my
way. Under a blaze of colored lights, to the
tune of "Sweet Rosie O'Grady" tigers, giraffes,
lions, horses elephants and other gayly painted
members of the animal kingdom were flying
around in dizzy circle, rising and falling with
mechanical precision in what was supposed to

be the equivalent of wild flight.

As I watched them flashing by on their never ending journey something caught my eye which instantly awakened more than merely passing interest. This something was a girl of thirteen or fourteen, sitting astride a ferocious tiger which, with uplifted, menacing claws, swayed backward and forward, as it whirled about the course. The object of my interest was out of sight almost before I had gotten more than a brief glimpse of her, but brief as it was it was sufficient to hold me there for further contemplation.

A mass of yellow curls bobbed up and down with the swaying of the feline steed and with each downward movement a short dress billowed up in the air displaying a generous expanse of flesh above the top of her hose.

I watched this seductive bit of feminity with increasing interest till the contrivance on which she was diverting herself came to stop and she clambered down, displaying further expanses of flesh and panties as she swung her leg over the back of the wooden effigy. Departing through the narrow exit, she ambled down a passage between two rows of ring throwing and other swindle schemes with me close at her heels and watching covertly over my shoulder, to see whether there were any parents or older com-

panions in the background. I saw nothing to indicate that anyone besides myself was interested
in her movements, and as she paused to inspect
a display of knick-knacks in a window I sidled
up to her and murmured in her ear:

"Having a good time, cutie?"

She looked me over appraisingly and with but
brief hesitation replied:

"Not very. Nearly everything's closed up."

"Like to take a ride on the roller coaster?"

"Sure!" was the succinct and satisfactory reply.

Something about this girl's appearance and the
matter of fact way in which she accepted my invitation, told me that I had a live one. As we
made our way to the coaster an adroit question
or two extracted the information I was most interested in, namely that she was alone. She lived
but a short distance from the park, and was in
the habit of coming by herself, to spend an hour
or two in the early evening.

Carefully I sized her up, and the inspection
tended to confirm my first estimate. Despite her
baby face, there was something in her eyes which
denoted sophistication. The dress she wore was
extremely short, and displayed too well a pair of
round, mature legs sheathed in glistening black
silk stockings, a luxury common enough now, but
rather unusual for young girls at that time. She

also had on high heeled French slippers, something still more unusual for extremely young misses.

When we reached the entrance to the coaster, I invested in a sufficient number of tickets to carry us around the track four times. The device in question commonly denominated as the "Russian Mountains" was an inclined track which ascended to an elevation of some height. Little three seated cars were drawn up this track, and permitted to descend a winding course under their own momentum. It was extremely popular with young couples, and it was quite permissible for a gentleman to put his arm around his companion, as an assurance of protection when the cars shot down the steep incline which gave initial impetus and velocity to the journey. Moreover there were several enclosed sections constructed in the form of dark tunnels, located at convenient intervals along the course. Under cover of the darkness so provided warm lips could be discreely kissed, and if the circumstances were favorable, caresses of a still more intimate nature might be indulged in. Naturally, I had all this in mind when I suggested a ride on the coaster.

A scarcity of customers that night resulted in our obtaining the exclusive occupancy of a car designed ordinarily to accommodate three couples. As we slowly ascended the steep incline, I put my arm around my companion's waist. When the car searted down the straightway, gathering velocity with every second, she squeezed up to me, with the customary simulation of fright.

The first time around I contented myself with warm kisses pressed on half parted willing lips in the darkness of the tunnels and caverns as we speeded through.

As we started on the second trip, I raised my arm over her shoulder and let my hand rest lightly over one of her small but firm little bubbies, and as no objection was made to the contact, I ventured a bit further, and squeezed it softly.

On the third trip around, this same hand was on the inside of her bodice over her bare breast instead of on the outside. Its mate was under the hem of her short skirt lying on the smooth skin just above the top of her silk stocking— and disposed to go higher.

On the fourth and final trip the hand last referred to had deftly found its way up the inside of a panty leg and was pleasant contact with something softly hairy, warm, and very moist.

All this had been accomplished with the complete acquiescence and entire complacency of the little miss with the baby face and woman's

legs. City girls are more sensible than country
girls.

When we got off the car I had such a hard-
on, I wondered uneasily whether poeople would
notice my pants sticking out in front.

How to bring this fortuitous encounter to a
satisfactory conclusion was the next problem.
And, in a flash, there came to my recollection
another charming feature of this amusement
park which also greatly contributed to its pop-
ularity with young couples.

This feature consisted of a tiny lake where row
boats were available for a shilling an hour. In
the center of this lake was a small island with a
bit of sandy beach and about its interior a few
trees, and shrubbery. It was toward this island the boats carrying amourous couples were
invariably steered and doubtless the trees there-
on could have told many interesting stories of
romances which had budded and come to flower
beneath their discreet shadows on summer nights.

Elated I turned to my companion and suggested a ride on the lake. She was agreeable, but
cautioned me that she must be home before
nine-thirty, or her father would come after her.
A hasty glance at my watch told me that it was
then almost nine-thirty, but unscrupulously, I
told her there was plenty of time. We hurried
accross the park grounds to the lake, and under

a string of lights hanging above a floating platform to which were anchored several dozen row boats I made the necessary monetary arrangements for the use of one of them.

The boatman winked knowingly at me as I helped my little friend to seat herself. Seizing the oars, I quickly had the small craft skimming over the water. The moon was in first quarter, softly illuminating the scene and a circle of electric lights around the lake twinkled brightly and were reflected back from the velvet surface of the water. I saw with inward satisfaction that there were no other boats out and unless some couple was already at the island we would have it to ourselves. I circled it once and found that, as I had hoped, it was unoccupied.

"Shall we rest a little while on the sand?" I insinuated softly.

"If you want to!" she answered, with a sly smile.

A bit of maneuvering and I quickly had the prow of the boat close against the sandy shore. I jumped out, pulled the small craft up on the beach, and assisted my companion out.

We sat down on the sand. I knew from what she had said about being home early, that we had no time to loose. Placing an arm around her I drew her down so that her head was resting on my lap. I bent over her and as I covered

her mouth with mine   I slipped a hand under
the edge of her dress, and up between her legs.
And a moment later one of my fingers was in-
sided the temple.

The road had apparently been traveled already.

"You'e had it before, haven't you, cutie?" I
murmured.

"Yes!" she replied shortly, her legs twitching
under the effect of my fingering, "Lots of times!"

"Who . . . ?"

"Oh, some boys I know!"

When I put my hand between this girl's legs,
I had first inserted a finger in her vegina to see
whether the way was "open" and after assuring
myself on this point, I withdrew it, and felt for
her clitoris, with the intention of exciting it. I
found, to my surprise that it was a great deal
larger than that of any female I had previously
manipulated. Also it was of a different shape.
Instead of being a small elongated ridge it was
conical in shape and stood up seemingly half an
inch or so. Under my touch it became perceptibly firmer. It was like a diminutive little
cock and it seemed to me the tip of it must
project out between the upper lips of her cunt.
Its likeness to a little cock was further apparent
as I continued to finger it, for it pulsed and
throbbed to the touch, standing out harder and

firmer. Absorbed in this unusual phenomena, I prolonged my digital examination, touching, squeezing, and feeling until my companion, frantic at the extended manipulation, exclaimed:

"I can't stand any more of that! Hurry up and let's do something!"

I straightened up and glanced out over the water. There was still no signs of other boating parties on the lake but the possibility that some might arrive at an inopportune moment suggested prudency.

"Let's go back behind those bushes," I suggested, "so that if anyone comes, they won't see us."

"All right!" she agreed, and jumped to her feet.

We retired to the relative seclusion of a clump of vegetation not far away, and which offered aslight shield from possible observation, there, raising her dress and holding it tucked under her chin, she began unfastening her panties.

As she fingered what seemed to me an interminable number of buttons, I dropped my knees and endeavored to assist in the operation.

Freed, finally, the garment fell to her feet and she kicked it to one side, at the same time twisting the lower part of her dress around her waist. It was a pretty picture, which revealed by the subdued light of a crescent moon as she stood there with her bottom, thighs and legs down to the tops of her silk stockings exposed to my eager eyes.

I was still on my knees before her, when yielding to a sudden impulse, I pressed my mouth to the exposed surface of her stomach, below her navel. The skin was so refreshingly cool and smooth that for some moments I continued ot caress it. Then I became aware of the contact of the softest and finest of silken hair against my chin. And with it came the sudden realization that this was a golden opportunity to try something which had long intrigued my fancy, a rare and precious opportunity, dropped right into my lap by the Gods of chance and good fortune.

My heart leaped with excitement, and without wasting a moment in speculation or deliberation I slipped my arms around her naked bottom, drew her closer, and ... pressed my mouth right over her moist little cunt.

As I did so, I felt her hands on my head, trying to push me away.

"What are you trying to do!" she gasped.

But my tongue was already inside the valley. Up and down between the wet lips it raced pausing finally to centralize its caresses over and around the odd, tit shaped clitoris. And, as when I had petted it, it responded by stiffening

out and increasing in size. I felt it throb violently each time my tongue passed over it, and my
own cock began to jump in sympathy.

I stopped licking it, and getting the tip between my lips commenced to suck it.

" Don't do that!" she gasped again, but there
was a strange disparity between her words and
actions, for now, instead of trying to shove me
away her fingers were entwined in my hair, and
she was pulling me to her and at the same time
had arched her body forward.

"Don't do . . . ah! Oh! Oh! Like that! Oh
that feels nice! Oh! Oh! Oh! Don't stop! Don't
stop!"

This clamor aroused me to a perfect frenzy,
and I redoubled my efforts, intending to make
her have orgasm once this way as quickly as I
could, and afterwards, put something bigger and
stiffer than my tongue into her.

Suddenly I felt the muscle of her thighs tense,
her clutch on my head tightened, I sensed some-
hing wet and stricky dripping from my lips and
chin, something which seemed to react on my
own sensibilities, and before I could rip open
the front of my trousers ejaculation was on me
and the semen running down inside my clothing.

About this same moment, my companion's
legs gave way beneath her, we were in a confused tangle of bodies on the ground, with her on

top. We lay still for a few moments panting, and when I recovered from the effects of my involuntary orgasm, I ruefully squeezed out the last few drops from my now willing scepter of pleasure and wiped it off wth my shirt tail.

She pulled her dress down over her naked bottom and stoop up.

"Hurry up!" she urged, "it must be nine-thirty, and my father will come after me."

"Gee! I wanted to do it once the regular way before we went back!" I protested.

She glanced uncertainly at something which was hanging limply and flacidly from my unbuttoned trousers.

'Your tiddie-widdie is all soft now. It won't go in that way. Will it get hard again?"

"Yes, if we wait a few minutes. It's still early."

"Well . . . if it doesn't take too long. Maybe I can make it get hard by jiggling it!"

Extending her hand she took the lethargic piece of flesh between her fingers and began to work the foreskin back and forth in an effort to restore its erectile inclinations.

She continued patiently, and in a few minutes I began to feel the first pleasant glow of awakening virility.

"Look!" she giggled, "It's getting fatter already! I do this to my brother sometimes. He likes it. I sneak in his room in the morning before he gets up. He pretends to be sleep, and I jiggle it until that white stuff squirts out!"

If anything had been lacking to quickly elevate my cock from its still rather sonomulent and recumbent position this opportune and disingenuous confidence fulfilled the requirement.

In instant response to the aphrodisiacal picture her words evoked it straightened out in turgid erection.

Spreading my coat out to protect her bottom from the rough ground I placed myself between her arched knees and a moment later, to the accompaniment of tremulous sighs and other expressions of delectation on her part, my cock was sliding back and forth between the tight folds of the mysterious domain which babies struggle to get out of and men pass most of their lives trying to get back into.

Resting my weight upon my hands on the ground, I looked down into the flushed face below. Her distended eyes and gasping breath told me that she was close to orgasm, and when a second later her legs flew up to clasp themselves across my back and her arms tightened around my neck I drove in the few final thrusts which were necessary to complete our mutual ecstasy.

Slowly I picked myself up from the ground.

We dusted and straightened out our disordered clothing, and returned to the boat.

No sooner had my companion seated herself than she arose again to exclaim in dismay:

"My panties! I forgot to put them back on!"

So back we went to where they were lying in solitary abandon, and as she stepped into them, I struck a match and glanced at my watch. It was exactly eleven o'clock.

"It's after nine-thirty now, isn't it?" she inquired anxiously.

"A little." I admitted.

Again we returned to the boat and were soon gliding shoreward.

"Did you like it . . . I mean that first way?" I asked, as I pulled at the oars.

"Oh, it was just wonderful! Nobody ever did that to me before" she added, giggling, "That's the way the French do it, isn't it? A boy wanted to do it to me once, but I wouldn't let him. I didn't know it felt so good."

"Well, we'll do it again some time, if you want to. You can meet me at the park, and we'll get a boat again."

"All right! And the next time you do it to me that way Ill . . . "

The phrase was never finished for as we approached the boat landing, the figure of a man detached itself from the shadows and came toward us.

"I'll bet that's my father!" she whispered uneasily.

A moment later she exclaimed:

"Why, it's my brother! They've sent him after me. Don't tell him we were at the island! If he asks you tell him we were just rowing around on the lake!"

Disturbed by her evident alarm I slowly guided the boat up to the anchoring platform. As she stood up to get out the brother, apparently a chap of about my own age, stepped up and exclaimed angrily:

"Where have you been all night?"

Without wainting for an answer, he seized her by the arm and glaring ferociously at me, hustled her off.

Chapter III

So pleasantly and agreeably had my first adventure in "frenching" transpired that whatever lingering doubts I may have entertained as to the esthetic considerations involved in the act were dispelled nor did I therefore permit fastidious scruples to deter me from taking entire advantage of such opportunities as came my way.

My experience and observation lead me to believe that the lingual caress is gratefully received by most females, although many through a feeling of shame, will protest hypocritically at first. Their opposition generally melts rapidly under a little persuasion, or perhaps the employment of just enough force to provide an excuse for submission.

Women are by nature more lascivious than men but the precepts and inhibitions which are inculcated in them from puberty to maturity, exercise a powerful restraint, and automatically assume a hypocritical prudery they may be far from inwardly feeling. Few are ever able to completely free themselves of the belief that this pretense must be maintained even with the men who receive their most intimate favors.

I shall insert here a few episodes which though out of the chronological order of events I have attempted to follow in this biography, will nevertheless not be miss as illustrations of the peculiarities I have reference to.

Once, under a temporary domestic arrangement, I lived with a girl of very ardent disposition, who lent herself enthusiastically to every erotic fancy our youthful passions could suggest, and we were neither of us novices exactly. There was, therefore, no logical reason for the slightest degree of prudery between us.

It was my custom to arise at seven o'clock in the morning, and in order not to awaken her I always dressed and shaved quietly, and slipped out with the least possible noise. One morning I left our apartment at my accustomed hour, ate my breakfast in a nearby restaurant and was about to proceed to my office when I discovered that I had left papers at the apartment which I should have brought with me. So I retraced my steps and, supposing that Gabrielle, my companion, was still asleep, I turned the key quietly, intending to slip in and get my papers without disturbing her.

The door to the bedroom was slightly ajar and as I put my hand on it to open it wide enough to permit my entry, a sight was unexpectedly revealed which caused me to remain where I was.

Gabrielle was awake, but she was not aware of my presence.

She had thrown back the bed covers, and with her night robe drawn up over her breasts was lying on her back knees drawn up and legs separated. One round white arm was resting at her side but the other, not so innocently occupied, was extended down over her abdomen. Her wrist was moving vigorously—and the tips of two fingers were lost to sight amid the glossy tendrils of hair at the base of her stomach.

In plain, vulgar, everyday words, my little Gabrielle was jacking herself off.

The sight reacted instantly and violently upon my own emotions. My first impulse, after observing the spectacle for a few moments, was to take off my clothes and delay my return to the office for half an hour or so, but it occurred to me that it might hurt her pride to know that I had witnessed her act, thinking possibly I had intentionally spied on her. But even as I hesitated undetermined, the episode came to a sudden conclusion. I heard a subdued gasp, the movement of her wrist was accelerated for a moment, then ceased and she relaxed languidly, closing her eyes. I slipped away from the door and quietly left the apartment.

The really curious termination of the incident referred to came a fortnight later. Business matters required that I make a trip from the city which signified three or four days absence from home. While I was discussing the matter with Gabrielle she remarked in a joking way that she didn't know how she was going to "get along without it" during the period of separation, to which I replied:

"Well honey, you can do what you did before you had me, can't you?"

She looked at me in a startled way, and said:

"What do you mean, Gilbert?"

"I mean, you've still got your fingers, haven't you?"

When the significance of my words dawned on her a wave of crimson passed over her cheeks and to my astonishment she exclaimed with great indignation:

"Why, I never did that in my life!"

"What! Never?"

"No! Never!"

"Not even once, honey?"

On another occasion I was discussing with a feminine acquaintance the subject of suppressed longings and inhibitions. She was twenty-five or twenty-six years old, had been married, but was separated from her husband.

I had expressed it my belief that there was

no person living, who did not carry in his or her heart a secret longing for some particular form of sexual gratification which had never been indulged, either because of lack of opportunity or inhibition through fear or shame. Something in the look she cast at me, or in the way she quickly averted her eyes, told me that in her case at least I had hit the nail on the head. Curious to confirm the supposition, I urged her to confess.

"Come now! Own up! Isn't there something naughty you've wanted to try for a long time, but never dared?"

She made no immediate reply but the color of her cheeks was proof enough of the accuracy of my surmise. It took a lot of coaxing and encouraging, but I finally got the story.

When she was seventeen, she had known a young man who courted her assiduously for a brief period. The courtship had not resulted in anything serious, although he was likeable young fellow. Later he moved from the neighborhood and she had never seen him again, though she remembered him with some affection.

Some years later and while married, she had a dream in which this young man figured prominently. In this dream she was standing naked before a tall mirror brushing her hair. While so engaged, he appeared in the room and kneeling on the floor before her he separated the lips of her genitals with his fingers and sucked her clitoris until she had or dreamed she had orgasm. And ever since, she had suffered an inordinate longing, a longing she had never before voiced, to have a man do it to her exactly as in this dream—she standing naked before a mirror, and he kneeling at her feet as she brushed her hair!

Needless to say, I volunteered to help her convert the dream into immediate reality, but no quicker were the words off my lips than with flaming cheeks she fled from the room, and locked herself in the bathroom, and it was half an hour before I could coax her to come out.

Here was a girl who for years had ardently and passionately longed for a certain form of sexual gratification and yet, when the opportunity was at hand, shame prevented her from taking advantage of it.

Later, I put my cave-man tactics of "take it first and ask afterwards" into effect, and had the satisfaction of "bringing" her several times in rapid succession by the famous French method, although unsupplemented by mirror or hair brushes.

Another instance of feminine curiosity which for naive simplicity and ingenuousness certainly took the prize, comes to my mind with the recollection of a little sixteen year old, whom I succeeded in coaxing into my room on several occasions while living in a boarding house her widowed mother presided over. Subsequently our meetings were effected late at night after the mother had gone to sleep, the girl slipping into my room when all was quiet in the house. She was an innocent appearing little damsel and I hesitated to take full advantage of the situation until I heard from her own lips that she had already been initiated, and by no other person than her own uncle—a man of forty-five at least, and who lived under the same roof.

According to her story, from the time she was eleven years old he had been in the habit of fondling and caressing her, and fingering her genitals. One morning, some months before I had made her acquaintance, she had gone to his room to awake him. He seized her, and pulled her down on the bed by him

"He pulled my dress up," she confided, "and unfastened my panties. And then he threw the covers off, so that he was all naked. His thing was sticking up, and he rubbed it between my legs. I tried to get away from him but he held me tight. And then he made it go clear inside me. I hurt awful at first, but pretty soon it began to feel kind of good, too. When he let me up there was blood all over my legs and on the bedsheet. He made me get a clean sheet and put it on the bed. And then he wrapped the bloody one up in a bundle, and hid it so mama wouldn't see it. And another time, one day when mama was gone, he did it to me again. He sat down in a chair and unfastened his pants and made me sit on his lap so his thing went up inside of me."

After hearing this interesting history I lost no time in breaking in on uncle's preserves, and thereafter on an average of once a week I enjoyed her company in the still hours of the night, while the rest of the household was wrapt in slumber.

On one of these occasions after she had slipped off her nightgown and was cuddled up in my arms, she whispered:

"If I asked you to let me do something to you, would you let me?"

"What do you want to do to me, sweetheart?"

"It's something . . . oh, you'll think I'm awful if I tell you!" and she hid her face against my neck and began to giggle.

My curiosity was aroused as it always is when I see a women giggling and blushing at the same time.

"I'm not easily shocked, sweetheart. What is it you want to do?"

"I won't tell unless you promise to let me first!"

Rather suspecting that I was destined to be the object of an amateur experiment in cock sucking, I assured her that I was willing to take a chance, and promised my acquiesence.

"Well, I . . . oh, I'm ashamed to tell you!"

Thoroughly intrigued, I encouraged her with caresses and coaxing. When the secret was out my surprise as it ingenuous, almost infantile nature was boundless. She wanted nothing more nor less than to masturbate me with her fingers so that, quoting her own words, she could "see it when it squirts out!" Speechless for a moment, all I could do was gasp.

"Is that all you wanted to do, sweetheart?"

Her eyes refused to meet mine, but she nodded her head.

"Well, there it is. Go to it!" and I turned over on my back.

With shining eyes, and flushed cheeks, she extended her hand, and began to work the foreskin up and down. All that was necessary for me to do to help her gratify her curiosity was to lie still and let nature take its course. And a few minutes later she was recompensed with the sight of half a dozen copious jets which suddenly flew upward from between her fingertips, and barely missed striking her in the face in their trajectory.

About the time I was nineteen, chance enabled me to witness something which made a deep impression on me and the recollection of which has always inspired me with a degree of caution and consideration with respect to the forcing on a woman, of any sexual act patently contrary to her inclinations. With this episode I resume the chronological order of my biography.

Shortly before my nineteenth birthday, a commercial establishment in Liverpool, which was indebted to my father to the amount of several hundred pounds, became insolvent and went into bankruptcy. There was a possibility that by being represented at the bankruptcy proceedings, a small portion of this money might be saved and unable to go himself my father delegated me.

Armed with the necessary documentations, and instructions as to my duties I boarded the Liverpool express. It was the first journey of importance I had ever made alone and I was highly elated. I had been provided with a sum in cash sufficient to defray my expenses for the week or ten days I would probably be there, and with the clever idea of diverting a good portion of this money to personal entertainment instead of going to a first class hotel as I had been instructed, I sought for and found a cheap place, where I could get lodgings for a third of the amount indicated for the purpose.

Although I did not know it at the moment, the place I had selected was a rendezvous for street walkers and prostitutes of low order, some of whom roomed there permanently, others utilizing rooms by the hour, or by the night. My ignorance of this situation was short lived for before a day had elapsed I had taken note of the larger number of females about the place and had observed that they came in accompanied by gentlemen, and went out alone.

This circumstance though intrigued rather than displeased me, and I kept my eyes open, observing with great interest all that was transpiring around me. The women for the most part were of a plane considerably inferior to that of the sporting girls I had come in contact with at home. They looked bedraggled, tired, unhealthy and I saw only a few who possessed attractive qualifications. Their attitude was bold, and I received several plainly worded invitations which, due to my somewhat fastidious taste in female merchandise, failed to awaken enthusiasm.

The second night I was in this place I overheard sounds emanating from the room next to mine, which excited in me a burning curiosity to see what was taking place. There was a connecting door between the two rooms and I examined it carefully to see whether I could find

a way to peek through. The keyhole was
securely plugged up. A streak of light was visible under the lower extremity of the door, but
all efforts to peer under this door were fruitless.
Meanwhile, the creaking of bed springs and the
murmur of voices increased my excitement. I
listened to these significant sounds, with my ear
pressed to the door for ten or fifteen minutes,
after which they ceased, the light under the
door disappeared and the sound of receeding
footsteps in the hall told me the occupants had
taken their departure.

I heard no more that night, but the next day,
just as I was about to enter my room the door
of the adjoining one opened, and a girl came
out.

She was a girl who might have been any age
between twenty-six and thirty, a girl who some
years previously had probably been possessed of
real beauty. She was slender, and the pallidness
of her face was accentuated by a heavy coating
of powder. Her lips were painted a too vivid
scarlet and the precisely drawn Cupid's bow
stood out in startling contrast with the whiteness of her face. Despite her garnish aspect,
there was still something attractive about her,
and her eyes, as she turned them momentarily
upon me, held a trace of sad wistfulness.

I heard her door open when she returned

about twelve o'clock that night, but this time she evidently was alone for I heard no sounds but found no way by which visual access to the room be secretly gained. But, while speculating on the subject, an idea occurred to me. The next day I located a hardware store and purchased a sharp pointed ice pick. That evening I waited until I heard her leave the room. Then I pushed the ice pick through the corner of one of the door panels. I did not dare to make a very large aperture for fear it might be observed, and had to trust to luck that the small perforation would enable me to see into the room when lights were on.

Intending to speak to her in the hall I loitered around the lobby for two hours the following evening, but she failed to put in appearance so I went to my room and tried to pear through the perforation in the door panel. The room was in darkness and I could see nothing. Profound silence indicated that she was not there and I wondered uneasily whether she had left the place for good. However, I decided to stay in my room and wait. I fastened a small piece of pasteboard over the hole in the door panel, so that the light from my side would not betray the stratagem in case she returned suddenly, and selecting a magazine from among a number I had brought with me I lay down to pass the time reading.

I had been sleeping some time when I became aware of the sound of angry voices. At first they scarcely penetrated my consciousness, but gradually I awoke to their significance, and just as I emerged from a state of nebulous uncertainty, into clear possession of my faculties I heard an angry male voice exclaim:

"By God, you will!"

The softer, but also angry voice of a female rejoined:

"I will not!"

Jumping from the bed I hurried on tip-toes to the door. The card I had pinned over the hole was still in place but I quickly removed it and applied my eye. For a moment my vision obfuscated by the light, revealed nothing, but as my sight cleared, a strange scene was presented to me.

In the adjoining room, accompanied by the girl I have previously described, was a big, bearded fellow in a sailor's uniform. The female was completely clothed, apparently exactly as she had come in from the street, except that she had removed her hat. The man was standing near her. The front of his pants was unbuttoned, and from the opening there projected in full erection, a cock which to my startled eyes appeared to be nine or ten inches in length.

The woman was standing before him in an attitude of defiance, her eyes blazing. From bits of the conversation, oaths, curses and threats which came to my ears, I gathered that he was trying to make her take it in the mouth and that she refusing the honor. It seemed that in his acceptance of her solicitation when she accosted him in the street he had stipulated the "French" method, she had said nothing to the contrary. Probably the poor girl expected to content him with something of a less disagreeable nature once she got him to the room.

"If you didn't want it that way why in hell didn't you say so?" he hissed, his face contorted with rage. "By God, you can't play me for a blooming fool!"

And then before my astounded gaze his hand suddenly shot out, and entwined itself in her hair. In grim silence, broken only by the scuffling of feet on the wooden floor, began a struggle which literally held me spellbound.

The woman fought valiantly to free herself, but subjugated by the cruel grasp of her hair was relentlessly forced to her knees. His fingers twisted themselves more firmly in her tresses and the next instant his cock was pressing and rubbing against her face and lips. She tried to evade the contact by turning her head sidewise but again his clutch on her hair tightened, and irremissibly, her face distorted with pain, she was forced to yield. Her lips parted and first the head of his cock then three or four inches of its length, disappeared between them.

Her head, imprisoned between his hirsute hands, was now impelled rapidly backward and forward, and between her distended lips that incredibly enormous cock slid back and forth.

I watched with bated breath, frozen, incapable of movement, my eyes glued to the tiny aperture.

Five minutes of more humiliation lasted. I perceived his body stiffen out in response to orgastic reactions; he forced as much of his cock into her mouth as he could and held her head still. From his rigid posture and the strained expression on his face, I knew that he was ejaculasting in her mouth. I heard some choking, gasping sounds, saw her eyes roll upward and fix themselves on his face and on her own countenance, pitifully pallid and distorted, such an expression of hate as I have seldom seen reflected on a woman's face.

His hands relaxed their grasp on her tresses, and he withdrew his cock from her mouth. It had already begun to lose its rigidity and was beginning to sag downward. As soon as she was released, she sank down on her hands and knees and began spitting out great mouthfuls of slimy fluid.

Paying no more attention to her, the man buttoned up his clothes, threw a few coins on the bed, and walked out.

She remained on the floor for several minutes after he had gone, spitting and hawking, then dragging herself to her feet, she went to a corner of the room beyond my range of sight. But I did not need to see to know what she was doing for the sound of splashing water, followed by a long period of gargling and spitting, spoke plainly enough of her effort to cleanse her mouth of the pollution to which it had been subjected. When she was again in my line of vision, she undressed and put on her nightgown. As she stepped to the side of the bed, her eyes fell on the coins which were still lying there. She picked them up, looked at them pensively for a moment, and then hurled them across the room. The next instant, the room was plunged into darkness. With muscles cramped and aching from uncomfortable posture, I too, slipped into bed, to lie awake until daylight, reviewing the sordid drama I had witnessed.

At the age of twenty-one, my naturally active disposition, coupled with requirements for cash now considerably in excess of the allowance provided by my father, impelled me to begin thinking of making my own living.

My father would have preferred that I continue my schooling a few years longer, but I was not of a very studious nature, and when he saw that I was determined he interposed no further objection and suggested a junior clerkship with the firm in which he was interested. This would have been an advantageous arrangement in many senses, but to me it had inconveniences. My father and I were of distinctly different types. His ideas were strict and inclined toward the puritanical. His constant reproval of what he considered dissipations on my part annoyed me vastly and interferred with my pleasure. The truth is, he never knew the half, but what he did know or guess was enough to maintain between us a certain amount of animosity. I was headstrong, resentful of any restraint and not wishing to be too closely subjected to his observation, declined the opportunity and announced an intention of finding something for myself. His skeptical attitude as to my capability to do this stung my pride, and made me even more determined.

For weeks I assiduously answered advertisements with no other results than a few fruitless interviews with firms which invariably required services of a nature which a lack of experience disqualified me from fulfilling, and then, when I was about ready to give up in despair, my efforts were rewarded. I was summoned to and obtained employment in the office of a well known financier, a man whose diversified interests extended across half the globe; banks in England and Scotland, diamond mines in Africa, railroads in South America. I was employed to act in capacity of personal assistant to this man, A little which though flattering of sound turned out in reality to mean nothing more than I was sort of glorified office boy and messenger. Nevertheless, the fact that my duties kept me in personal contact with the great man, gave me a certain prestige not enjoyed by other employees, most of whom occupied positions of far greater importance.

My employer turned out to be a man of quick and irrasible temper. His depreciative, and often unnecessarily offensive criticisms soon inspired me with a cordial dislike for him. However, I put forth my best efforts, constantly endeavoring to please him, and before long I began to sense the fact that I was rising in his estimation. Within a short time more important duties were being confided to me, though curiously enough, as his confidence in me increased, my antipathy toward him also grew space and I came to despise him whole heartedly for his arrogance and boorishness.

One afternoon when I returned after executing an errand which had taken me to a distant part of the city I saw a young woman leaving his office. With an ever appreciative eye for feminine pulchritude, I appraised her trim figure, gowned with the simple elegance which bespeaks both taste and wealth. My gaze, starting at the faultlessly shod little feet traveled upward, and rested on a face of such marvelous beauty as had seldom been my lot to behold.

I have always been a bit more partial to brunettes, than to light complected women, influenced possibly by the popular superstitution that brunettes are more passionate than blonds, a supposition which experience has demonstrated to me without foundation. In this instance however, my inclinations suffered a sudden reversal. The young woman on whom my attention was blond. A blond whose skin was the texture of flawless immaculate ivory; whose tresses, visible below the brim of a fashionable little toque, clung around her ears and neck in ringlets of spun gold and in whose violet tinted eyes was reflected all the glorious splendor of ardent young womanhood. In brief the most exquisite, the daintiest, the most seductive bit of feminity imaginable.

For a few fleeting moments only was I permitted to regale my eyes with this delectable vision, and then it passed from my view.

"Who is she?" I gasped, addressing my inquiry to a nearby clerk.

The fellow turned a fishy eye on me and responded superciliously:

"No! If I knew I wouldn't be asking. Who is she?"

"She's the chief's wife."

More questioning of other employees evoked supplementary information. Our employer had married this girl about four years previously; she was of titled parentage and in her own rights.

My admiration, based on nothing more than one brief glimpse, grew to infatuation. Past loves faded into insignificance, and never did I more ardently long to possess a woman than I did this one. As my mind became more and more obcessed with the infatuation, my dislike for the man who was the rightful possessor of this gem of loveliness increased and for the first time in my life I felt the stinging lash of dominating, unrestrainable jealousy.

I learned that on some occasions she came to the office, and day by day I looked forward to another glimpse of her, with hungry anticipation. It was two months before the longing was gratified, and then I saw her again. She was, or so seemed to me, even more lovely than I had first imagined and so rapt was I in the contemplation that my attitude was observed by other employees and after she had gone I was forced to listen to many jibing witicisms.

During several succeeding weeks I ceaselessly dreamed and thought of this woman, not with exception or hope, but with that blind adoration which finds its only solace in silent, unrequited worship. I had brief glimpses of her once or twice a month, and ultimately it seemed to me that as her glance momentarily met mine, there was an expression of understanding in it, as though she felt, or divined my adoration.

I had been working for nearly a year when my employer summoned me to his office one afternoon.

"Gilbert, here is a little matter I want you to take care of. The wife's private secretary is away on a vacation, and until the girl returns, I have instructed her to send for you once a week to assist her with the household accounts."

The electrical effect of this communication upon me may be easily imagined. At last! An opportunity to be near, if but a few moments to the hitherto unapproachable Goddess of my dreams. I could scarcely conceal my elation as I assured him I would be delightful to be of service to his wife. But how delightful he certainly did not suspect.

It must not be supposed that I was beguiling myself with any fantastic hopes. No; for once, and despite the success with which most of my previous amorous campaigns had been waged, I was infatuated with a woman I considered far beyond my reach. To me she was little less than a deity; the possibility that she might descend into my sphere of life and being was not entertained even in my wildest dreams. The lines of caste are well defined in England. She was the essence of aristrocracy; I was a plebian, completely outside her world. I expected nothing.

Six days later a message was laid on my desk requesting me to report at the house.

A taxi conveyed me through the city's most exclusive residential section, along flower bordered streets under leafy bowers of foliage, and I shortly had my first glimpse of my employer's residence. It was a veritable castle of stone architecture, almost concealed under climbing ivy beautiful vines and trees.

In answer to the clang of a heavy brass knocker, appeared a trim, luscious little maid gowned in a short black dress, over which a white lace edged apron was neatly draped. Her plump legs were admirably displayed in glistening silk and these, together with other obvious charms would have captured my heart in a minute, if it had not been otherwise occupied to fullest capacity.

Upon being informed of my identity, she ushered me into a reception hall, and while I gazed with admiration at the tasteful splendor, she went to notify her mistress of my presence.

On the interview which followed I shall dwell but briefly for intoxicatingly pleasurable as it was to me nothing transpired which fits well into this naughty biography. In the intimacy of the small study to which my employer's wife conducted me, she seemed more delectable, and desirable than ever, and it was with the greatest delight I found that my presence would be needed once a week during the absence of the secretary. The work was nothing more arduous than the figuring of domestic accounts, the writing and recording of checks issued in payment to merchants, and represented less than two hours of time. At its conclusion she called the maid requesting that I be served with refreshments, and shortly thereafter I departed. During the interval we had been together her attitude toward me had been friendly, but entirely impersonal.

Four successive visits transpired, during which I feasted my eyes and tortured my soul with more or less surreptitious contemplations of her charms. On the fifth, last, and epochal occasion of our meetings, I was conducted into the little private study as previously and was soon engaged in putting the domestic accounts in or-

der. It was to be my last visit, for the absent
secretary was returning in a few days, and there
would be no further occasion for my presence.
The object of my idolatry entered the room and
seating herself in a huge leather cushioned chair
near me, began to look over the tradesmen's bills,
initialing them one by one, and handing them to
me to be recorded for payment.

Glinting under the rays of sunlight which
filtered into the room, through the interstices of
lace curtains, golden ringlets of hair, tied with
a single ribbon at the base of her neck, rippled
down over shoulders and back in riotous profusion. Draped loosely about her body, was a
dressing gown or lounging robe of black velvet,
trimmed with a fringe of pure white ermine down
the front and around hem, sleeves, and neck.
This strikingly beautiful garment was not buttoned, but was sustained with a silken girdle
carelessly knotted about her waist. In a sitting
posture the lower edge of this robe hung just
below her knees, and her legs, visible from the
knees down, were clad in the sheerest of silken
hose through whose translucent weave, the snowy
whiteness of flesh beneath was discernible.

The combination of circumstances that day
seemed to have been arranged painstakingly by
Destiny. Or did the lady herself have a hand in
the arranging?

The intimate garment, her closer than usual proximity, the casual touch of a strand of hair light as thistle down against my cheek as the leaned over me to make an observation about an entry in the small ledger, all contributed to provoke in me a veritable torment. The room was scented by some perfumed essence emanating from her hair, body and garment, the air was vibrant with an undefined but palpable atmosphere of eroticism.

The chair in which she was sitting was one of those heavily padded, amply built affairs with an inclined back. A slight frown passed across her face as she glanced over a bill from an establishment which supplied most of her wearing apparel. I paused, waiting for her to conclude her examination of the account and as I waited, my eyes fixed on her she changed her position slightly raising one of the silk clad legs across the knee of its companion.

In the position in which she was sitting, she was not fronting me directly but rather to one side. The movement she made in crossing her legs caused the folds of the lounging robe, loosely tied, to separate slightly and bulge outward above the cord around her waist. And through the aperture so fortuituously provided, immediately became visible an exquisitely rounded breast of alabaster whitness, crowned with a tiny rosebud nipple.

Seemingly she wore no undergarment beneath the fur trimmed robe! And as though this entrancing sight were not enough to suffocate me with emotion the raising of her leg had also elevated the border of the garment and above the purple silk band which supported her hose, a brief space of naked thigh was visible. Those bits of white flesh held my gaze like magnets, and with my eyes first on one, then on the other oblivious to everything else in the world, I continued to look, and as I looked a thought involuntarily formulated itself in my mind.

"I'd give a year of my life just to put my mouth on her cunt!"

A prolonged silence suddenly impressed itself upon me and brought me back to earth. Guiltily I raised my eyes to hers. Those violet eyes instead of being fixed on the bill in her hands were contemplating me in a speculative, half sardonic manner.

Guessing that she was conscious to some extent of my emotion, the blood rushed to my face.

"What are you thinking about, Gilbert?" she asked dryly, while the ghost of a smile hovered about her lips.

She looked at me, apparently surprised at the

ingeniousness of my answer and then suddenly broke into peals of silvery laughter. Relieved but still greatly embarrassed, I sat in silence, hardly daring to meet her gaze. When the laughter subsided she laid the bill down and murmured in a low, insinuating voice:

"Gilbert, what would you do for me?"

"Anything!" I answered fervently and without hesitation this time.

"Anything!"

"Anything?" and the word was repeated with a slow, deliberate insistence which I comprehended held some special significance.

I looked at her intently in an effort to divine her meaning, but though there was a smile on her lips the violet eyes were inscrutible.

"Anything!" I repeated, putting all the emphasis I could into the all embracing word.

Chapter IV

There was an interval of silence, unbroken except for the tapping of the pencil she still held between her fingers, against the edge of the table. Her gaze now turned from me, and through half closed eyes she seemed to be looking off into space lost in introspection. She had not changed her position, and though she must now have been aware that intimate portions of her body were visible to me she made no effort to conceal them from my view.

There was no longer any doubt in my mind that this situation was replete with glorious possibilities and though I hardly dared venture a guess as to what might be in store my heart was pounding with anticipation.

Her eyes, which for some moments had been fixed unseeingly on the curtained window, were again turned toward me. From her lips fell the softly spoken request:

"Sit down by me here, Gilbert."

And she motioned toward the rug at her feet.

I needed no second invitation, and rising from my chair I accommodated myself on the soft rug. The bit of snowy flesh above the top of her stocking was now so close to my eyes, that the faint, blue tint of a tiny vein, which traversed the rounded curve of that immaculate limb was perceptible.

She extended her hand, and I felt her finger tips running through my hair, caressing my forehead, and temples. The intoxication of her nearness, the subtle perfume which emanated from her body, the exquisite intimacy, all contributed to embolden me. Reverently, but without hesitation, I doubled back a portion of the fur trimmed gown, exposing her leg from the knee half way up her thigh, and laid my lips upon the cool flesh. It was as smooth in texture as the finest silk.

The play of her hands over my hair and face continued, but otherwise she remained motionless under my caress. On the firm, smooth skin I pressed kiss after kiss. My hand itched to raise the brief fold of garment just a trifle higher but something counseled me to hold myself in check, and let her take the lead.

I heard a sigh fall from her lips. She withdrew her hand from my head and shifted her position. She had been half sitting, half reclining with one leg crossed over the other, and when I had taken my place at her feet I had seated myself close by the side of her legs. But now she lowed the leg which had been crossed above its companion, and at the same time moved her body in my direction so that I was directly in front of her knees, instead of at one side. The dressing robe, already well elevated, was pulled tighter by this movement, and further expanses of alabaster whiteness were revealed.

I looked into her eyes in an effort to read her wishes. She smiled faintly in response, and her fingers engaged themselves in the knot of the silken cord which girdled her waist. It was unfastened, and with one sublimely indifferent gesture without hesitation without the least semblance of hypocritical prudery she flipped the folds of the garment back, exposing her nude body to me in all its splendor.

Scarcely breathing, my whole being submerged in an ecstasy of delight before this extraordinary spectacle of celestial beauty, my gaze traveled up and down over her naked form from the tips of daintily and exquisitely molded breasts, over the smooth, slim waist and stomach to where a softly rounded promontory, covered with the silkiest of little curls and ringlets of gold, heralded the proximity of the temple door.

Many a naked woman have I seen, both before and since, but never have I seen the physical perfection of this woman duplicated. Perhaps after all there is something in aristocratic blood different from that possessed by those of more lowly birth.

Silent, apparently indifferent to my rapture, she passively permitted me to feast my eyes freely upon the spectacle of her nudity.

Now, she moved her limbs again, so that one of her knees was on either side of me. Again she placed her hand on my head with a touch which gently, but unequivocally bid me draw myself closer. What I had viewed before, while her knees were still close together had been sufficint to hold me breathless, but what was now revealed was of a nature to inspire thoughts other than those of mere admiration for physical perfection.

Beneath the mons veneris, with its soft curls and ringlets, there now appeared, frankly and clearly, the coral folds of flesh which constitute womanhood's supereme treasure. So small and virginal in aspect were the petal-like lips, that it hardly seemed possible they had everbeen distended by the intromission of a male organ.

Deliberately, she let her body slide lower in the chair until her thighs were extended well out beyond its edge, the flower of her sex close to my face, her legs widely separated on either side of my body.

I knew now what was expected of me.

The wish I had so fervently voiced to myself,

the favor I had vowed to be worth any price, was about to be granted me.

I rested my cheek for a moment against the satiny flesh of one of her thighs. Then, I pressed my lips against her mons veneris. The hair felt as fine and soft to the touch as that of a new born infant. Then, quickly and expertly, my tongue sought out and penetrated the perfumed valley below. And, an instant later it was playing over her clitoris with all the fervor and agility at its command. A slight sound issued from her lips—something between a gasp and an exclamation—and she shifted her body forward a bit to better accomodate me. Then silence, profound and absolute.

Under the spell of one of the most intense erotic intoxications I had ever experienced, I plied my tongue feverishly, first centralizing its activities upon her clitoris, then, up and down the length of the gental cleft, and even inside the vaginal aperture as far as I could project it.

But a few moments of such energetic stimulation as I was subjecting her to would have had most women squealing and kicking, yet I failed to observe in her any of the customary reactions. I glanced upward toward her face. She was lying with her head thrown back, her eyes were closed and her countenance as calmly reposed as though she were sleeping. Not a gesture,

not a facial expression, not a sound or movement
to suggest that she was under the influence of
any emotional stress. Her hands rested quietly
on the heavily padded leather arms of the chair,
her little, tapering fingers curved lightly around
them.

This was something of a new experience for
me, but I had received several surprises that day
and I did not pause to analyze the apparent
anomaly.

Applying my mouth more firmly against the
coral folds I succeeded in getting her clitoris
compressed between my lips and then imparted
a vigorous suction to it. Almost instantly, the
hitherto motionless form began to show signs of
life. I felt vibrant tremors in the flesh of her
thighs where they pressed against my cheeks
and perceived the muscular contractions of body
and limbs as her physical organism began to
yield to my ministrations. Maintaining her clitoris a prisoner between tightly compressed lips,
and without relaxing the suction I was applying to it, I again glanced upward. Her eyes
were wide open, distended, and fixed upon me
with the intent, strained expression of approaching orgasm. The slender fingers, which before
had rested idly upon the arms of the chair, were
now clenched tightly around them.

My own passions augmented by the knowledge

that she was near the verge of orgasm, I slipped my hands under the cheeks of her bottom and pressed her closer to me. This movement brought a quick response. There was a violent, spasmodic shivering in the thighs which were compressed about my cheeks, and a sudden flow of moisture bathed my lips. The pressure of her thighs increased for a moment, and then relaxed. I felt her fingers on my forehead, pushing me away. I arose to my feet, trembling from the effects of the intense stimulation. Again she was lying with head thrown back, eyes closed. Except for the rise and fall of heaving breasts she might have been one of those exquisite, little tinted porcelain statues, one may sometimes see in private collections in Holland— jewels of erotic art in which no tiny detail of life and color is omitted. The heaving of her breasts subsided. The violet eyes opened, and scrutinized me quizzically.

"Was that what you were thinking about, Gilbert?"

And then, little tapered fingers closed over the edge of her gown drew it around her naked body, veiling it forever from my view. A short lived romance was over, and as I look back over the span of years, it still seems more a dream than a reality.

In the early part of the year 1922 my grandmother died in Scotland leaving estate, bequests in money to various members of the family including myself, and shortly thereafter I received as my share the tidy sum of one thousand pounds sterling.

This unexpected acquisition of ready cash made possible the realization of a dream I had long entertained—a visit to Paris. My father tried to dissuade me, urging the desirability of investing the money in some manner calculated to assure my future. But as in the past, I paid little heed to his counsel and proceeded with my plans. I had heard and read of wonderous things to be seen, and enjoy in the French capitol, and was avid to experience its delights in person.

With two hundred and fifty pounds in my possession, I embarked for Paris. I had studied the French language in a desultory fashion and although I could not speak it with any degree of fluency I knew enough to understand and make myself understood.

The visitor in Paris with money to spend has no difficulty in discovering ways to spend it and people anxious to assist in the task. Indeed they seem to gravitate toward one as though literally endowed with some uncanny instinct for smelling money and had it not been for a most fortuituous accident, the relatively small amount of money with which I was provided, would have been greedily snatched from me, without having sufficed to cover a fraction of the programe I had outlined. The accident referred to, was the chance meeting of a British friend, some years older than I, and well versed in things Parisian. He was on the point of returning to England, but before departing he gave some pertinent advice about trusting myself to affable strangers, and introducing me to a member of the French Sureté, or Secret Police, who, during his hours of leisure, which seemed to be plentiful, was disposed to act as a confidential guide and companion in consideration of a modest fee.

And a better guide it would not have been possible to find for not only did this man know every inch of Paris, but his presence assured me respect, and protection from impositions. He understood English fairly well, and we formed a sincere friendship.

In his company I began to learn something of the real Paris night life—not the flambouyant surface, with its imported American jazz orchestras, etc., but the secret undercurrent, which only the initiated could penetrate. My new companion was familiar with secret resort from the lowest and most abject dens of vice in subterranian cellars to luxurious temples located in respectable appearing edifices, scattered through the city.

On the occasion of one such outing, I struck up an acquaintance with a well dressed cultured gentleman who like myself was unaccompanied. We had a few drinks together and the man, evidently taking a liking to me, invited me to accompany him the following evening to an exclusive club in which a motion picture was to be displayed. He had seen the picture once, but was so impressed with it, that he wished to see it a second time. I was much interested, for I had not as yet had an opportunity to see a picture of this nature, so gladly accepted his invitation, agreeing to meet him the following evening.

Half afraid that his friendship had been born of the numerous libations we had shared, and that it would be forgotten before the birth of a new day, I was early at the prearranged meeting place. My fears were unfounded, for punctually at the hour agreed, he appeared.

We ate dinner together, and when it was concluded, we took a taxi which turned so many corners I quickly lost all sense of direction. We wound up finally in a quiet street, and came to a stop before a large stone edifice which, as far as its outward appearance indicated, might have been the residence of some banker or retired politician.

A touch of the bell, a few words exchanged between my companion and the doorman, we were inside. Turning our hats and coats over to an attendent, we proceeded down a hall which led us to a spacious saloon, in one extremity of which was a stage. Comfortable chairs, lounges, and sofas were distributed about the place, in number suffiient to accommodate a hundred or more guests. At the moment of our entry, the saloon was lighted and there were, between men and women, some sixty or seventy persons present.

I glanced around curiously. This was clearly a place of the elite. The women were gowned in the height of fashion and most of the men were in formal dress. Colored liquors were being served in thin long stemmed glasses and as my companion and I crossed the room toward an unoccupied settee, he was greeted familiarly on all sides.

As soon as we were seated I began a survey of the feminine element and quickly observed that among the women present, were many both young and beautiful. The entire lack of formality and constraint, the freedom of their movements, the generous display of breasts, backs, shoulders and legs was suggestive of the demimonde, and I could hardly restrain a feeling of envy toward the men whose company they shared. In imagination I followed them after the conclusion of such entertainment as this we were about to witness to luxuriously appointed apartments where with sense aflame, they abandonded themselves to wild orgies of lust.

As my gaze wandered from face to face it came to rest upon a young woman of rare and striking beauty over whom a vapid faced Frenchman was hovering and showering with exaggerated attentions. The woman I guessed to be in the neighborhood of twenty-five. She was dressed in black, and the front of her gown was cut so low that it barely reached the nipples of two singularly large, and beautiful breasts, whose upper halves were entirely exposed. Always an admirer of pretty breasts, this exotic charm alone would have been sufficient to engage my attention. Her figure was slim, a fact which further accentuated the prominence and contour of her breasts. Raven black hair threw the pallor of a face of lily-like whiteness into sharp contrast. She did not look French and my impression was that she was Italian or Spanish.

There was something violently sensual about this girl and my pulse quickened as I watched her. My companion broke into my absorption with a dry commentary.

"You seem to be interested in the Russian."

"Russian?" I replied, "I thought probably she was Italian. Whatever her nationality is, she is a remarkably beautiful woman."

"I know her well enough to present you if you wish. Russian nobility but better fixed than most of them, who have come in since the war. Married a rich Frenchman when she was fifteen. Too fast for the old fellow. Caught her in "delictu flagrante" and divorced her. But he settled an annuity on her that will keep her in luxury as long as she lives."

His comments augmented, rather than diminished my interests, and I assured him I would be very glad to make her acquaintance. Whereupon he led me across the room and after obtaining the lady's permission, I was duly presented.

To my delight, the Russian girl had a good knowledge of English so I was spared the ordeal of trying to converse with her in French. She introduced me to her escort, who acknowledged the courtesy with little cordiality and glared at me with a look which seemed to say:

"I'll thank you to kindly get to hell away from here."

However I did not permit his coolness to interfer with my efforts to make myself agreeable to the Russian girl, whom I found to be even more fascinating at close range than at a distance. She was a woman who exhuded sexual magnetism from every pore, one of those women seemingly designed by Nature to appeal to men's sensual appetites—women born to be dolls and playthings of men rather than wives and mothers.

In the midst of our conversation we were interrupted by a bell announcing the beginning of the picture, and the lights were suddenly extinguished. The four of us groped our way through the semi darkness toward an unoccupied settee and sat down, the Russian girl taking her place between the Frenchman and myself.

The picture which was shown, was of a startling and realistic nature, dealing with the methods and operations of white slavers recruiting girls for houses of prostitution, and the violation of one of their innocent victims.

First appeared upon the screen the copy of an advertisement, which translated to English, read about as follows:

WANTED—Girls for dancing and theatrical work. No previous experience necessary. Salary paid while learning. Apply at . . .

Then was shown a cheaply equipped office, in which a long line of girls stood waiting their turn to make application for the promised employment. Behind a desk a man was sitting, interviewing the girls one by one, filling out a card with the applicant's name and address, with notations as to age, whether living alone or with parents or guardians, and data as to the applicant's characteristics and appearance. Each was asked whether in case of acceptance, she would be agreeable to leaving the city. As quickly as this data was jotted down the applicant was dismissed with a statement to the effect that she would be notified later as to whether she could be placed.

The object of this preliminary was to enable the slavers to select attractive girls and by their adroit questions determine which of these would be the safest subjects for exploitation.

The next episode of the picture finds us viewing the humble quarters of two Parisian misses, evidently sisters, living alone. We recall having observed the younger of the two girls in the line of applicants before the psuedo theatrical agent's desk. She is a pretty, beautifully formed little blond of innocent, almost Madonna-like features. The furnishings of the room through neat and orderly, indicate resources of the most modest nature. At the moment the scene is flashed before us, the younger girl, clad only in a chemise which permits us, to admire a pair of round shapely legs, is engaged in washing some stockings in a porcelain basin. The elder, dressed for the street, is apparently about to leave when a knock is heard at the door. On the threshold stands a sleek shifty faced individual. He glances at a card in his hand and inquires whether this is the domicile of Mademoiselle Eva Thibault. The object of his inquiry, listening to the conversation from behind the door, hurries to drape her naked limbs, and when this is accomplished the visitor is invited to enter.

He is pleased, oh, very pleased, to announce that Mademoiselle Eva has been selected to play a small part in a musical revue, which is to open within a week at Bordeaux. She must prepare to accompany him immediately as some days will be necessary for the young lady to familiarize herself with her part. They are to take the train this very morning and she will greatly oblige him by making immediate preparations.

The modest habitation is thrown into a fever of excitement by the news of this good fortune and the two girls throw things right and left as they hurriedly pack a small grip with articles of appeal and toilet for Eva's use, while the gentleman obligingly waits outside.

In a very short space of time Eva is dressed and packed and ready to accompany the agent. An embrace and exchange of kisses, an affectionate farewell, and the sisters part.

Eva, accompanied by the agent, enters a waiting cab.

When we see them again, they are leaving the train, presumably at Bordeaux. Another taxi is called and an address given. Now we are taken to an edifice of gloomy aspect, located in what was probably in days gone by a part of the city's residential section, for the house, grey, weather beaten, dilapidated, is crowded in between a warehouse and a brewery. The windows are closely shuttered and at first glance it seems to be an unoccupied building.

The taxi bearing Eva and the agent now appears and stops in front of this structure.

As they alight Eva glances wonderingly about her but still in the eager enthusiasm of her prospective rise to fame and wealth behind the footlights she suspects nothing and lends herself docily to the machinations of the widely procurer.

They ascend the steps, the man explaining that this a boarding house in which arrangements have been made to house the members of the cast during their stay in the city. He rings a bell, and after a long wait the door opens sufficiently to permit their entry, and closes behind them.

Eva is in the trap.

They are confronted by a heavy faced woman

of curiously masculine aspect. She is stoutly
built and extremely dark and heavy eyebrows
give her an ominously sinister appearance. If
it were not for her ponderous breasts and enormous hips, we would suspect this personage of
being a man dressed in female apparel. Eva is
presented to her as one of the "new girls" and
acknowledges the introduction timidly. The
woman places an arm about her with exaggerated familiarity and assures her that she will like
the place, and that they are going to be great
friends, both of which statements we doubt very
much.

The agent and the woman now withdraw a
few steps, and converse in whispers. A roll of
bills changes hands. The man, with a cynical
smile on his wolfish features, tell Eva that the
"madame" will take care of her from now on,
bows and retires. His work is finished.

From this point on the tragedy unrolls with
precise and startling realism.

We see Eva, looking curiously about her confused and timid in the strange surroundings,
conducted to an interior room in which are lounging half a dozen other girls in intimate dishabille. Several of these are probably no older
than Eva but they do not resemble her in appearance. They are heavily rouged and painted,
their faces denote hardened sophistication, their

eyes are bold and hard. In fact, they look like typical prostitutes of the cheaper class. A brief pause in this room while Eva is presented to these young ladies. They watch her silently, with much the attitude of a feline watching a mouse as it ventures out of its hiding place. She is hurried into another apartment. Here the madame invites her to remove her cloak and hat, and informs her that a lunch will be served her.

A table is prepared, and a slovenly servant appears with food and drink. Eva eats a few mouthfuls and is urged to take a glass of wine to refresh herself from the journey. Within a few minutes after taking a portion of the liquor offered, her head begins to droop. She tries to straighten up, an expression of fright crosses her face, but the drug she has unknowingly consumed renders her powerless and she falls sidewise in her chair. Like a hawk, the madame is upon her and seizes her just in time to prevent her from falling to the floor. Lifting her as easily as though she were an infant, she carries the unconscious girl from the room, up two flights of stairs and into a small alcove, windowless except for a glass skylight overhead.

Eva is now in drugged stupor, her eyes are closed, her form limp and yielding. Her hair, which has become unloosened, falls in a golden cascade over her shoulders. The madame lays her upon a bed. She stands for a moment looking down on the unconscious child. What thoughts are passing through her mind, as she gazes upon that innocent face? Does she feel a pang of remorse for the pure beauty which is to be offered up on the altar of lust? Or is she simply calculating the probable profits which will accrue to her, through the defilment of that lovely body? Most likely the latter, for her face betrays no indication of pity, but rather gloating satisfaction, as she proceeds to disrobe the girl. First she removes the little high heeled slippers, then the filmy silk stockings which on being withdrawn disclose a pair of white symetrical legs upon which we have previously gazed. Now, lifting the girl to a sitting posture, she draws up and removes her outer garment. Then follows a short underskirt, a chemise, a dainty brassiere, a pair of little silk panties, and Eva is disclosed to us in all her virginal nudity.

With the last article of clothing removed the madame pauses again to examine the prostrate form. Leaning over it she feels the diminutive but plump little breasts, as though to prove their firmness. Her hands descend, she seizes the child's knees and pulls her legs apart. The next instant her finger is inserted within the sexual cleft. The expression on her face indicates that she is pleased with the result of this profane exploration. Eva's maidenhead is intact and will bring a lucrative return in cash. She gathers up the girl's clothing, and taking it with her leaves the room, locking the door behind her.

Outside the door she stops, slides back a small panel, and stands for an interval peering through this aperture at the girl, still lying motionless and unconscious upon the bed. She closes the panel and proceeds downstairs.

Now we see two persons engaged in telephonic conversation. One of these is the madame. The other is a man of middle age whose face bears the stamp of dissipation and cruelty. The printed text in French tells client, of a new acquisition, of superlative charm, and virginal integrity. The gentleman is being offered Eva's maidenhead. An appointment is made, and the picture dissolves from our view.

A sign is flashed upon the screen announcing a five minute intermission and the lights are turned on. During the course of the picture which I have briefly outlined, and which consumed possibly some thirty minutes in the showing, the Russian girl had remained silent. Now she turned to me with a smile, and inquired as to how I was enjoying the picture. I replied that it was very impressive, more so as it was the first film of this nature I had ever seen. She seemed surprised and began to question me as to how I had been entertaining myself while in Paris. I mentioned a number of the places I had visited, and found she was familiar with most of them.

"Do you know," she broke in, irrelevantly, "you're quite good looking?"

Somewhat taken aback, I replied with assumed seriousness.

"And not a bit conceited!" she continued, smiling.

Further conversation was interrupted by a bell which announced the continuance of the film, and the lights were again turned off.

It is now night, and we return to the room in which Eva, victim of white slavers, is held prisoner. Eva, naked, is sitting on the edge of the bed, weeping. In the position in which she is sitting, directly before us, we are able to appreciate her physical beauty in all its extension. Between her slightly separated thighs, below a little cluster of golden curly hair, the flower of her sex is partially visible.

The scene is emotional, and not a sound is heard in the saloon except the whirr of the film as it is fed into the projecting machine.

Under cover of the darkness, the Russian girl places her hand upon my knee. Her fingers squeeze the flesh lightly and the contact sends an electric thrill vibrating through my body.

Between this, and the effect of Eva's nakedness, my cock begins to harden. I sense its rapid increase in size under the constriction of my clothing. The hand upon my knee begins to travel upward, and comes to rest exactly over the spot where my clothing is most distended. And through the texture of the garment, the clasp of warm, soft fingers becomes apparent. I drop my hand down over hers, and press it expressively.

The picture changes, and we are taken to another room in which the madame and the hard faced man we previously saw at the telephone are in conference. They sit on either side of a small table, between them a bottle of wine and glasses. At intervals script in French conveys to us the import of the conversation, which revolves about the price of Eva's maidenhead.

"Are you sure?"

"I couldn't get this in!" replies the woman, holding up the index finger of her right hand.

"Well, how much?"

"To you, five hundred francs."

"Five hundred francs?" exclaims the man, angrily, springing to his feet, "Five hundred francs? Too much!"

"Five hundred francs." replies the woman, stolidly, "Five hundred to you. A thousand to anyone else. I can get it. She's the prettiest little piece you ever laid eyes on. Breasts like this . . . " and she cupped her hands expressively.

"I won't pay it!"

"Come and look!" answered the procuress, cunningly, rising to her feet.

The man glared at her a moment in silence, then he too arose, and followed her.

They proceed to the room in which Eva is confined. The small panel is slid back, and the man peers through. For a long interval he stands motionless, his gaze riveted on the spectacle of Eva's nudity.

"I'll pay it!" he whispers, closing the panel.

They return to the room in which we previously saw them, and the man removes a wallet from his pocket, counts out the stipulated amount, hands it to the madame, and in return receives the key to Eva's prison.

They drink a glass of liquor to the successful termination of the transaction, and the madame, with a suggestive leer, wishes him a pleasant night.

Across the screen appears another notice, announcing a brief suspension of the picture in order to present a symbolical dancing act or terpsichorean fantasy entitled "Deux Femmes Moderness."

Short, but spectacular, it brought enthusiastic applause from the audience. Across the stage, now bathed in a flood of changing lights of red, green, violet and gold, whirled two beautiful young girls, except for hose and slippers, strip stark naked. More than naked, for the black silk hose accentuated a hundred fold the white nudity of their torsos. In an embrace so close they seem but one body, they writhe, twist, undulate and whirl about the small stage.

The flashing lights and the shifting melody of color lend an erie fantastic effect to the nude bodies difficult to describe, while their close knee to knee, thigh to thigh, breast to breast contact, on every fiber of the sensual emotions. Their steps increase rapidity; one places her knee between the legs of her companion, their movements become so swift the eye can scarcely follow them. Dizzily whirling, pirouetting, literally flying, under the changing colors of the spotlight they seem like the weird figures of an erotic dream.

So close did they maintain their embrace during this striking and really beautiful dance, that not for a single instant had their sexual parts been visible, but their undulations, the interweaving of thighs and legs was highly suggestive and the emotional effect upon the spectators was apparent.

Thee exhibition reaches its climax with one of the dancers swaying backward, supported by the arms of her companion who lowers her to the floor and then throws herself upon the recumbent figure with wild, and frantic lust. The bodies blend together as mouth to mouth, breast to breast, and clitoris the Sapphic union is consumated.

The applause is generous and most of us would have appreciated an encore, but the dancers, after acknowledging the applause, stand for a moment facing us, favoring us for the first time, with an unobstructed view of their lithe bodies, then run behind the curtain.

The stage is again in darkness. The white curtain is lowered, and before us appears the lustful, cruel face of the man who has paid five hundred francs for Eva hymen. He stands, rapt in ecstatic lubricity before the door of the room in which she is confined, peering through the secret panel at the girl who, unconscious of his scrutiny, is lying naked on the bed, her face covered with one white forearm.

He closes the panel, and inserts the key in the lock of the door. Eva hears this sound, as the door opens, she springs from the bed.

"Oh! Who are you?" she gasps, too terrified for the moment to remember her nudity.

The man, as though unwilling to lose a single detail of the delicious spectacle, closes the door behind him without removing his gaze from her body. He stands there gloatingly feasting his eyes on the delectable vision of her young loveliness until Eva, awakening suddenly to the significance of his steady gaze seizes a sheet form the bed and jerks it toward her in an effort to drape her naked body.

Something in the eyes of the man standing before her acquaints her with the desperate nature of her circumstances, and of the futility of words. She darts across the room, beats the wall with her fists, screaming:

"Help! Help! Help!"

Chapter V

Up to this moment he had simply stood looking at her, and even now, as she beats upon the wall with her fists and desperately calls for succor, he makes no effort to silence her. When, breathless and exhausted, the first furor of her efforts to secure the protection which would never come had died down, he said:

"Calm yourself my little beauty. There is no use yelling. Nobody can hear you. This room was fixed especially for noisy little girls."

Eva stares at him wide eyed with terror, and he continues:

"It isn't going to hurt! Be nice, and I'll make you a pretty little present! Look . . . and thinking to awaken her cupidity, he withdraws a roll of currency from his pocket. But ah, not all the money in the world would have impressed Eva in this moment. Trembling like a frightened dove in a trapper's hands, she thinks of nothing but the security of her little room in Paris. She stares at him uncomprehendingly, and again raises her arms to beat upon the wall.

"Come! Come!" exclaims the man, now beginning to show annoyance, and at the same moment he lunges toward her.

Eva shrieks, slips from his grasp, and starts toward the other side of the room. The covering she had draped around her body trails on the floor about her feet. She steps on it in her flight, trips, and falls on her hands and knees. In the confusion, the treacherous folds fall open, revealing her round white thighs, and naked bottom. Galvanized to action by the sight, her persecutor moves swiftly and before she can get to her feet, lifts her, kicking, struggling and screaming, in his arms. Carrying her across the room he sits down on the edge of the bed, and holding her on his knees, strips the sheet from her clasp and throws it aside.

"Now, little wild cat, kick and squeal till you get tired!"

Eva's frantic efforts to liberate herself from his clutch avail her nothing; he subjects her as easily as though she were a babe in arms. Nevertheless, she continues to struggle until her strength is exhausted. Finally, she relaxes. Her eyes close, and from beneath their lashes, big tears emerge, and trickle slowly down over her cheeks.

"Now you're coming to your senses. There is no use fighting. You'll like it after you've had it once!"

Gloatingly, he passes a hand over her firm

little breasts, and down over the smooth surface
of her stomach and thighs. Eva remains motionless in his arms, apparently in a state of apathetic
surrender. But suddenly she becomes aware of
a profane hand insinuating itself between her
legs. Again she comes to life, and with renewed
energy endeavors to defend the sanctity of this
most intimate part of her body. A hopeless effort, for the man, his passions aroused by the
sight and contact of her naked body rudely
restrains her, and imprisoning her two wrists in
one hand, forces his knee between her legs to
separate them. Having accomplished this, he
places his free hand squarely over her cunt.

Eva lies in his arms, rigid, frozen, her eyes
wide and staring. The hand of her tormentor
begins to move back and forth. He is rubbing
and squeezing her genitals—genitals which never
before had known the contact of a male hand.
And now, a coarse finger in inserted between
the scarlet folds. After a momentary exploration it is withdrawn. A smile of satisfaction
crosses his face. The madame has not deceived
him. The entrance to Eva's vagina is sealed so
tightly that scarcely his finger tip can be introduced within the tiny aperture.

The man-tiger is mentally licking his chops
in anticipate of the feast he is about to enjoy.
He lays her upon the bed, and begins to divest

himself of his clothing. Coat and vest are laid aside, shoes are unfastened, and removed. He strips off his shirt, trousers, underwear. His hairy formidable body is now in complete nudity. An enormous cock, foreskin draws back, and head exposed, projects in rigid, menacing erection.

Eva, unwinking, pertified, her face a frozen mask of terror, seems to see without comprehending. He advances toward the bed. She recoils to his touch and throws herself to the opposite side of the bed, moaning:

"No! No! No!"

He seizes her in his arms. There is a confusion of kicking legs and naked forms. Eva is making a last and final effort to save herself from the ignominious violation.

Her strength is not equal to the task. In a last gesture to protect her sexual flower from the enemy, she manages to twist about under her assailant, and lies upon her stomach, face down, legs tightly locked together. The man, aroused to a fury of lubricity by her desperate resistance, mercilessly pulls her legs apart, and places himself on his knees between them. The last defenses are going down. He slips his hand under her abdomen, lifting her so that her bottom is projected upward. Eva clutches at the iron frame of the bed, then, as her grasp is torn away, at the mattress, the coverings . . . but her strength is gone. Her body yields. Her face is buried in the bed coverings, but her hips, supported by the arm under them are elevated in the air and between the cheeks of her bottom something hard, rigid and hot in prodding, searching . . . he is going to put it in her from behind, dog fashion.

He lifts her bottom a bit higher and presses his hairy legs closer to the white flesh. The hand under her stomach is feeling and groping. He is endeavoring to place the head of his cock in the strategic spot.

"No! No! No!"

"Oh! You're hurting me!"

"Oh, don't! Please don't!"

And her exclamations rise to a shriek of anguish, indicated on the screen in script, beginning with small letters, which increase in size, terminating in immense figures which cover half the screen.

He has found the entrance and has forced the lock. Withdrawing the arm which has previously supported her he clutches her by the hips with both hands. With the shrieking girl now impaled, he begins the motions of copulation. His thighs recede from her bottom, and several inches of his cock are visible. He shoves it back in again pulling her bottom toward him at the same time forcing her to reciprocate his movements. And so, alternately pulling and pushing at the girl's bottom, he consumates the violation. At the conclusion we see him straining and puffing as he brutally forces the instrument of torture entirely wthin Eva's tender flesh. She hangs limp and motionless in his grasp, and when he releases her after the final culminating trusts she sinks back unconscious upon the bed, and the screen is darkened.

The spectators, impressed by the terrible realism of the representation, whisper hushed commentaries. The cheer is again illuminated, and before us, bowing and smiling, we see Eva, the madame, the villian, and the false theatrical agent. They disappear one by one, leaving Eva until the last. Smiling, she raises her dress waist high. There are no undergarments to obstruct the view. With her dress elevated fan-wise on either side of her, she undulates her hips with circular, rolling movements, projecting her genitals outward voluptuously. Then she drops her skirt, kisses her fingers to us daintily, and disappears.

We arose to take our departure, and as we did so, the Russian girl whispered:

"Come and see me tomorrow afternoon!" and at the same time a diminutive card inscribed with her name and address was slipped into my fingers.

I went.

And as a result of this visit, an invitation was extended to me to pass the fortnight as a guest in the beautiful little villa overlooking the river Seine, occupied by Irma, the Russian girl.

The invitation, tendered for a fortnight, was extended over a period of three months and constituted for me a species of scholarship and post graduate course in all the arts vices and aberrations of love. Before I had been with her a week I discovered that in comparison to Irma I was the veriest novice. There were depths of sensualism, psychic effects, mental aphrodisiacs, the like of which I had never dreamed.

The girl had taken a fancy to me—and proposed to "educate" me in accordance with her own theories, ideas and fancies. She was of strong will and dominating character, accustomed to indulge every whim, and to gratify every desire. Her religion, her very life, was sensuality. The villa was adorned with paintings, photographs and statuary of an erotic nature, veritable gems of lewd art. It was a treasure house of pornographic literature such as I had never laid eyes on. Histories, novels, biographies, and even transcripts of testimony in judicial cases involving celeorated sexual crimes. She possessed a collection of strange and curious devices designed for the provocation, or gratification of lust. In fact there was enough material here to have stocked a regular museum of erotic art, artifices and literature.

The uses to which some of these objects were destined were obvious while others constituted for me, complete mysteries. Irma, encouraging me to try to guess their uses, laughed heartily at my conjectures.

In contrast to this antiquity, I was intiated in the mysteries of some far more modern inventions—one of which was nothing more or less than the well known electric vibrator, or massage machine, such as may be found in any well equipped barber shop. Often indeed, had I enjoyed the refreshing sensation of a facial massage without suspecting the hidden potentialities of this apparatus. The rubber vacuum cup, vibrating under the impulse of an electric motor, placed over a woman's clitoris, or on a man's cock, will produce orgasm in less than thirty seconds if the vibration is not interrupted. And as if this were not enough an attachment has been provided by some genius, which may be substituted in female use for the vacuum cup. This attachment, available in five, six, seven, and eight inch lengths, is made of pliable rubber in shape and exact appearance, a replica of the masculine organ. In use, a condom is slipped over it for sanitary purposes. The effect upon a woman of this artifice is fulminating, and if orgasm is to be delayed, the vibration must be discontinued at short intervals.

Amongst other novelties of a more or less artistic nature, or untilitarian purposes, all designed to excite or gratify the passions, was a series of phonograph discs. One of these records oralized and reproduced in sound the courting, seduction and deflowing of a young girl by her sweetheart. Indiscreetly, she accompanies him to his room, "to see some pictures" he wishes to show her. Indignant at the nature of the pictures she reprimands him for his temerity, but under his coaxing and blandishments, she relents, and through the medium of words sounds exclamations, protests, all faithfully reproduced, even to the creaking of bedsprings, as she finally submits to his embraces, we participate in the invisible romance, exactly as though, veiled by a curtain from our sight, it were transpiring in the same room with us. Another, of a still more emotional nature, a rendition so true to life as to cause one to wonder whether a real rape had been consumated to effect it, oralized an assault upon the person of a young maid by a wandering vagrant. As he makes his way thru a lonely wood we can hear him soliloquizing to himself and lamenting the fact that he hasn't sufficient money to compensate female companionship, after having undergone a prolonged interval of enforced chastity in the provincial workhouse. At this point he spies a country maid, whose path, fortunately or unfortunately accordng to the viewpoint across his own. He detains her and endeavors to secure her complaisance with false promises of generous reimbursement. The terrified maid declines his proposition, whereupon he seizes her and to the accompaniment of shrieks, sobs and supplications on her part and lustful observations on his, he tears off her clothing, and rapes her.

Yes, Irma's hobby in life was sensualism. She had two favorite theories. One of these was that in order to hold a man's erotic fancy, he should rarely be permitted to attain orgasm in intercourse. Her reasoning was not altogether erronous, for it must be confessed that the masculine interest diminishes with satiety. The woman who can excite a man's emotions, and maintain them in a state of excitation, without permitting him complete gratification will not quickly lose her hold on him, but the difficulty is to find subjects who will submit to such machinations, for as is evident such a system requires the co-operation of the gentleman.

I was to a limited extent versed in the practise

and knew the advantages of holding back until my partner had reached the limits of her orgastic powess, but Irma carried the theory still further, sustaining in effect that even after the female was completely satiated ejaculation or orgasm should be avoided by the male, thereby maintaining an unsatisfied sexual urge which tend to fan, instead of extinguish, the fingers of passion. She showed me some very interesting articles on this subject but while I agreed with her in theory it seemed to me an impossible proceedure in actual practise. Nevertheless, I had no objection to lending myself to a few experiments along this line.

Irma initiated me in many intriguing aspects of psychic effects and though she frequently had to scold me for "letting go" when under strict orders not to do so, I must admit, that in following her ideas I enjoyed some of the most delicious hours of my life. And yet I realized that the effects over by considerable length of time, of the sustained, and prolonged excitation would be enervating in the extreme, and beyond the average man's physical capacity to withstand.

Irma was an ardent enthusiast of variation, but had a strong predilection for "frenching" and I passed hours at a time, with my mouth over her clitoris while the intimate caress was

compensated with her own warm lips encircling
my cock. She was an adept in the use of those
subtile, perfumed preparations for intimate feminine use and not once did I place my mouth on
her cunt without finding it fragrantly scented.
Ordinarily, she did not permit me to ejaculate
in her mouth, her customary proceedure being to
terminate the love bout when she preceived that
I was unable to withstand the caress any longer.
And more than once, after I had brought her
several times in succession, and had myself arrived at the ultimate stage of my powers of resistance, she disengaged herself from my clasp,
and went to sleep while I, with my cock still
vibrating expectantly, was obliged to forego
the satisfaction. It peeved me mightily at first,
but after a while I found that, as a stimulant
to increase and intensify the passions, this method was superlative. Girls, it's a wonderful system, and if you have the will power and the
determination to hold a man to it you can keep
him dangling from your apron strings indefinitely.
We men are curiously ungrateful creatures, and
the more liberally you treat us, the quicker
we are satiated. It's not the female who generously surrenders herself to a man's every whim
and fancy, who can long hold him, but rather,
the calculating, understanding female, who
knows how to keep him in a continuous state of

sex hunger. And the hungrier he's kept the firmer the anchor.

One of Irma's charms lay in the uncertainty of her determinations. I never knew from one moment to another what was coming next.

Surprising revelations as to how young maids comport themselves in boarding schools!

The lightness with which this kind of play was looked upon may be judged from the following: An English girl named Mercy, daughter of a wealthy British importer of tobacco, received naughty pictures and novels by post from a girl in Paris. One day, between the pages of a novel received from this source, she found a "french letter" or condom. This interesting but under the circumstances entirely useless gift was passed from hand to hand amid general laughter. A few nights later, another girl, a lively little French mademoiselle upon turning back the sheets of her couch preparatory to retiring, found between them a banana of ample dimensions over which the rubber condom had been stretched.

Brandishing the rubber clad banana in her hand, she announced that she was going to "get" the girl she suspected of perpetrating the joke. Accompanied by several of her friends Rosita slipped into the dormitory where the object of the intended assault was just getting into bed.

Waving the banana in the girl's face she exclaimed:

"Just for this, I'm going to fuck you!"

"You're not going to fuck me!" was the defiant answer.

A tussle began, which, because of the determined resistance of the prospective victim, might indeed have been lost by the French girl, had not her friends reluctant to be defrauded of the spectacle, come to her assistance. Between them they straddled the protesting, one out upon the bed, and held her while the little mademoiselle made good her threat.

"And I was one of the girls that held her legs!" added Irma, laughing at the recollection.

She entertained me with various anecdotes of her experiences with girls and women and seemed amused at my surprise at the ease with which she aparently found females willing to participate in such adventures. When she stated that there was an unlimited supply of them from the age of ten upward, my amazement gave way to incredulity. I could scarcely give credit to the assertion and yet before many hours had passed I was afforded an opportunity to judge for myself. For the following afternoon while driving leisurely about she pointed toward a group of small girls carrying baskets of violets, and smilingly referred to our conver-

sation of the previous evening. Often enough
had I observed these pert little youngsters, and
had been annoyed more than once by their persistent efforts to sell me flowers but their extreme youth made it seem to me improbable
that aside from selling violets, they had other
professions.

"Do you mean to tell me that those little girls
. . . ?" I exclaimed, incredulously.

"Every last one of them," she replied, "I'll
get one to come to the house, if you want me to."

"Get one!"

"Allright! Wait till I see one I like!"

Ordering the coachman to circle the block we
again approached the same group and we came
alongside of them Irma motioned the driver to
stop and leaning from the window she called
to one of the youngsters, a bright eyed, piquant
faced child of twelve or thirteen. The little
girl rushed up to her expectantly, and extended
tray containing a quantity of violets in little
bunches. Irma selected one eyeing the child
attentively the meanwhile, and gave her a small
coin. Then, removing a card from her purse,
she pressed it the child's hand and whispered:

"Come and see me to-night at seven o'clock,
darling!"

The girl glaced quickly at Irma, then at the
address on the card, then at me, back again at

Irma, nodded her head, and backed away.

"Of course, she'll come," replied Irma, dryly.

And, as punctually on the hour as though she had been waiting outside for the clock to strike seven before presenting herself, the child was at the door. She wore a fresher dress, and with all the inmate, and natural coquetry of a born Parisienne she had made infantile efforts to beautify herself.

Irma took her hand and led her inside.

If she was impressed by the luxurious, and exotic surroundings she did not show it although she gazed with interest at the little statues, pictures, and paintings with which the room was adorned.

"What is your name, darling?"

"Lucille, at your service, Mademoiselle."

"How old are you, Lucille?"

"Twelve years, Mademoiselle."

"Who do you live with?"

"With my mama, and my sister."

"How old is your sister?"

"Ten, Mademoiselle.

"Does she sell flowers, too?"

"Yes, Mademoiselle."

"Can you stay all night?"

"Certainment! If you desire, Mademoiselle."

"Very well, Lucille. The first thing we are going to do is to take a nice bath in the pool together. Then we'll have dinner and afterward we'll have a fine time. You can sleep here and go home tomorrow."

"As you please, Mademoiselle." was the courteous answer.

Placing an arm abut the child, Irma took her to the big bedroom, and while I lounged in the doorway, an interested spectator, the two undressed. When Lucille's garments were removed down to her little panties, she glanced uncertainly toward me, but Irma reasured her.

"Never mind him, darling. He's a nice man."

Off came the small garment, and Lucille was naked in the presence of her hosts. Like them, this child was immature. Only the hint of a round swell surmounted with tiny nipples marked the budding breasts. No shadow of hair was visible on the elevated prominence above her little cleft. Here again after many years, I saw another fat lipped, naked little "V" with its vertical incision and cute little dimple.

Irma herself was now disrobed, and before my sight was a vision in contrasts of female nudity. in the bold nakedness of childhood, the other in the full bloom of enchanting feminine maturity.

With soap, perfumes, and towels, followed by me, they proceeded to the tiled pool, and soon immersed in the limpid waters. After fifteen or twenty minutes of splashing and laughter, during which Lucille was diplomaticly rubbed, scrubbed, and sponged, they emerged, and after drying themselves Irma perfumed and powdered the child's body, dried her hair, and dressed her in a pajama suit which, though large, was pressed into emergency duty. Then she brushed and arranged Lucille's hair, tying it with a pink ribbon and finally, with her own toilet accessories, she first powdered, then touched up the juvenile cheeks with rouge. With a lip-stick she traced a dainty Cupid's bow upon the little mouth. The deft touches produced a complete transformation and I could harly restrain an exclamation of amazement at what water, soap, powder, perfume, lip-stick and rouge could do to a ragged younster.

During dinner I could scarcely take my eyes off of her, so incredible was the transition. She, except for brief replies to our questions, ate in silence. The mother, from what we were able to gather, was or had been a prostitute, Lucille and the younger sister referred to being the fruit of transcient amours, fathers unknown. Now they lived entirely upon what revenue was derived from the sale of flowers, and on what "rich ladies" gave Lucille and her little sister.

My curiosity as to what proceedure such children followed to please the "rich ladies" was unbounded. After dinner was concluded we went into the lounging room and here, after a few minutes, Irma left us, telling me that I might "play" with Lucille, but not to "hurt" her.

As soon as we were alone I took her upon my lap, where she sat passively while I loosened the belt of her pajamas. Slipping a finger between the lips of her cleft, I made discreet exploration. Her maiden head was intact and technically at least, she was a virgin.

Irma returned, drapped in a kimona. She lay down on the big, plush covered sofa and called Lucille to her. The girl lay down by her, clasping her arms about the recumbent form and their lips united in an amorous kiss. From this on Lucille calmly took the initiative. She continued to caress her older companion and finally slipping one of her soft little hands inside the breast of the kimona, she exposed Irma's bubbies, and applied her lips to the nipples of each in turn. With close attention I watched this tender play, while Irma lay still surrendering herself to the child's ministrations. Young as she was, she had acquired, or possibly it had been born in her, a skill and artfulness beyond description. Her caresses were as light and soft as the touch of a feather. While I watched I began to get a better comprehension of certain things which had formerly mystified me.

•

Like a humming bird flitting from flower to flower, the moist, red lips were being applied first to one, and then to the other, of Irma's snowy breasts. I saw the nipples stiffen out, and erect themselves as the provocative caress reacted magically upon them. Lucille clasped her lips over one of them and raised her head. The nipple slipped back with an elastic little jerk when released. She moistened the nipples with saliva, then twirled them between her finger-tips, until under the tantalizing manipulation, Irma began to twitch and tremble.

Beneath the kimona, which still draped her lower limbs, her thighs slowly separated themselves. As though waiting for some such indication the girl instantly threw the garment open, slipped one of her knees between Irma's thighs, bringing it up in close contact with her cleft. In this position, crouched over the naked body of her friend she hesitated glancing toward me as though doubtful as to whether she should proceed.

"Hurry up, darling!" gasped Irma.

Chapter VI

Without further hesitation with a matter of fact directness which indicated perfect familiarity with the task in hand, she twisted about on the sofa and the next instant her face was between Irma's legs. With my gaze now on Luiclle's bobbing head, then on Irma's face as she surrendered her body to the intimate caress, I watched the realization of the act following every graduation of its effects upon Irma in her facial expressions. When I saw her hands suddenly dart to Lucille's head and perceived in her eyes that intent strained look which preceeds orgasm I was almost on the verge of spontaneaus ejaculation myself. When the tensed thighs relaxed their pressure upon the child's face and the hands withdrew from her head she sat up, reached for a towel and wiped off her lips. Irma lay with her head thrown back and eyes closed for a few moments and then with a lanquished movement drew the kimona about her naked legs. With a sly glance toward me she placed an arm about Lucille and drew her face down, whispering something in her ear.

Lucille slipped off the sofa and approached

me. Before I had time to guess her intent, she stripped open the front of my trousers, withdrew my cock and standing between my knees, began to masturbate me. As the tide rose in response to her soft manipulation I made no effort to restrain it and sending the impending crisis, she cupped one hand over the head, and the other slowly drew out the semen. It spurted into her hand, tricking between her fingers in milky jets. When it was all out she wiped her fingers and then with professional seriousness, performed a like service for me.

"She's a perfect little jewel, isn't she?" said Irma, her eyes on me, a quizzical smile on her lips.

"She's a treasure!" I agreed fervently "I'd like to adopt her permanently."

"Well, we'll keep her here tonight, anyway. I want another session or two with her yet tonight myself." responded Irma.

We lounged there for an hour talking, joking and sipping burgundy while Lucille, over her first feeling of restraint, entertained us with accounts of her adventures with "rich ladies". We induced her to remove her pajamas and show us some of the positions and methods she was familiar with.

"Doesn't doing such things make you feel

funny down here?" I asked, placing my hand over her little cunt.

"Certainment! Sometimes the ladies do it to me, too!"

"Ah! How do they do it, darling?"

"Viola! With their tongues! With their fingers!"

"Does it feel nice?"

"Yes! It feels good down there, and all down inside my legs! Sometimes I do it to myself, too!"

"Show us how, darling!"

"With my finger! Like this . . . !" Suiting action to word, she pushed away the hand with which I was caressing her, spread her legs apart and placed the tip of a little forefinger on her clitoris, rubbing it with a circular motion.

She realized the exhibition with such an entire lack of self-consciousness, and in such a natural, matter of fact way, that Irma and I were both convulsed with laughter.

"Come on; let's all go to bed. You can show us some more there", exclaimed Irma when we had recovered our composure.

Carrying Lucille in my arms, I followed Irma to the bedroom. They proceeded to make themselves comfortable on the big bed where I joined them as soon as I had undressed.

Despite the outlet to my passion which

Lucille's slim little fingers had afforded but a short hour previously the sight and contact of the two naked females soon restored my virility, and wakened new temptation. I pressed up against Irma but when she felt my cock touch her bare flesh she jerked away.

"The way you are now," she exclaimed, "you'll go off before you've had it inside half a minute and I don't want you to. You've got to hold yourself! The way I feel tonight, I want a good long one, two or three hours, anyway!"

"But Irma, dear, I'll hold back as long as I can!"

"If you'd do like I tell you, you could hold back still longer and it would feel twice as good. But you won't do it, you wait just so long and then you let go!"

"But sometimes I can't keep from it!"

"That's just imagination. You don't try. If you'd stop moving it at the right time and be still you could be with a hard-on all night, and we'd have lots more fun."

"Yes, but when I get to a certain point I can't help but move it!"

"I'll fix you so you won't move it!" she exclaimed suddenly.

Jumping from the bed, she ran out in the room, to return a moment later with some twisted silk ropes she had pulled from a set of portieres in the drawing room.

"What are you going to do with those?"

"I'm going to tie you up with them."

"Tie me up?"

"Yes! Tie you up!"

"Go ahead!" I replied, much amused.

She pushed me down on the bed, obediently, I extended my arms and legs. First, she knotted the silk cord around one of my wrists and tied it to one of the corner posts of the heavy bedstead, repeating the process on the opposite side with my other wrist. Then she fastened my ankles in a similar fashion to the foot of the bed. When she had finished the job to her satisfaction, I found myself spread-eagled out in a position far from dignified but I consoled myself with the reflection that a good stout jerk would break the cords and release me at any desired moment. For the present I was content to let her go ahead with her play.

She surveyed her handiwork speculatively for a moment, and then began to laugh.

"Now I've got you just the way I want you, and this time, when you start squirting it will be when I want you to!"

During the tying-up process my cock had wilted, and now, pointing at it she addressed

Lucille who up to this moment had stood by, an interested spectator, only.

"Make the lazy thing stand up, darling!"

Sitting down on the edge of the bed near me, Lucille extended her hand and her fingers closed around the object referred to. A few movements of her wrist sufficed to restore its rigidity whereupon Irma, to my disgust, halted the pleasant manipulation. Accommodating herself on the opposite side of the bed, she began to discourse on the advantages of self-control, and the art of prolonging erotic pleasures, punctuating her remarks at intervals by reaching over and pumping my cock. It was a tantalizing situation in which I found myself—straddled out on my back, my arms and legs tightly secured, my cock pointing toward the ceiling and throbbing impotently under the provocations of the two females, who took turns in toying and teasing it.

But this was nothing in comparison with what was yet to come.

At Irma's suggestion Lucille got up on the bed and seated herself astride my chest, her knees doubled under her on either side of me and her cleft within a few inches of my face. The sight of this tempting morsel so close to my lips, the feel of her bottom on my chest and the pressure of her thighs combined to aggravate my condition.

"Now you can pay her back for what she did to me!" insinuated Irma.

More than willing, I raised my head, Lucille edged up closer, and in a few seconds my tongue was between the two little naked converging lips. I located a tiny clitoris without difficultty, and quickly demonstrated the fact that little clitorises are as responsive to an active tongue as big ones. And while Lucille was twitching and quivering with her genitals planted firmly over my mouth, Irma intermittenly pumped my cock, working it vigorously for a few seconds, then releasing it to throb helplessly in solitary abandon Lucille suddenly inclined herself forward, and I left her thighs clenching themselves tightly about me. She clung to me rigidly for a moment and then jerked away. She had received her compensation.

The taste and humidity of her genitals remained on my lips, augmenting my own excitation. Irma's hand was clasped about my cock, but she was not moving it. I raised my lips in an endeavor to obtain sufficient friction to release the pent up tide, but she divided the purpose, laughed, and withdrew her hand. Hungrily, my eyes devoured the lascivious spectacle of her nudity, and as they rested inevitably upon the most intimate of her charms, she murmured teasingly:

"You've seen hers, and now you want to see mine, too, eh? Viola! I'll let you look!"

And mounting on the bed, the exhuberant Russian placed herself on her hands and knees directly over my face. With all the desperation of Tantalus, grasping for water just beyond his reach, I strained my neck in an effort to reach her cunt with my tongue.

"Ha!" she exclaimed, "You're not satisfied with seeing it! Now you want to lick it! Well, lick it, then!"

And she sat down on my chest, as Lucille had done. And, as I had done with Lucille I did with her. I licked and sucked until she too had orgasm, and bathed my lips and cheeks with her offering to Venus.

This was the final straw and I decided that it was time for me to get a little satisfaction myself. I pulled tentatively at the cords and when they failed to give I jerked at them with all my strength. To my surprise I was unable to break them and after a few more efforts while Irma and Lucille looked on laughing I discovered that I was trussed up far mare efficiently than I had first imagined.

Irma assured me that she didn't propose to free me for "hours and hours yet" and that I might as well make up my mind to stand it.

In part, she made good her threat, and during

two solid hours, or more, I was subjected to such tantalizing manipulations and treated to such spectacles as nearly set me frantic. While I lay there alternately swearing and coaxing, she and Lucille diverted themselves in my sight by running the gamut from Lesbian and Sapphic embraces, to mutual mastubation, pausing between whiles to sit on the edge of the couch, and tease me with naughty words and actions.

About twelve o'clock, it became apparent that Lucille was exhausted, and Irma considerately carried her to an adjoining room, making her comfortable for the night. The younster had conscientiously lent her little body to every caprice of her hosts, and had well earned whatever recompense awaited her on the morrow.

Returning to where I was still stretched out on the bed Irma stood looking down at me a moment.

"Now see if what I told you isn't true!" she said.

She got upon the couch, and placed herself on knees astride my body. First came the contact of soft hair as she nestled down upon me, then the warm, humid constriction of her genitals as she sank down upon and received the scepter of life between her thighs. Once, trice, thrice I perceived a muscular contraction, as though something inside was convulsively gripping and squeezing the sensative gland. Then without conscious volition on my part, the semen was suddenly leaping forth to the grateful pressure. Jet followed jet, while she sat there immoible, her eyes fixed intently on my face. Not until the flood had spent its force was she caught in the current of its contagion. Then, raising and lowering herself on the impaling shaft with frantic energy, she gasped:

"Didn't I, ah! . . . tell you it was, oh! . . . better this way . . . oh! . . . oh! . . . o-o-o-oh!"

The fly in the otherwise delicious "ointment" was this: My little Russian sweetheart was a drug addict.

My lack of experience in such things prevented me from recognizing this circumstance during the first week we were together. She was young, possessed of great vitality and as yet her physical health had not been undermined. After I had gotten an inkling of the truth she discontinued all effort to conceal the addiction from me and tried to persuade me to experiment with narcotics, ridiculing my objections. So persistent were her efforts to conceive me that knowing her determined character, I was uneasy. I began to understand her phenominal sexual prowess, and the sudden furious accesses of lubricity which took possession of her, body and soul, at frequent intervals. I began to fear that I was permitting myself, unconsciously, to drift into swirling currents which eventually I would find myself incapable of resisting. I enjoyed all these things, but I wished to remian master of my vices and not become subservient to them.

One night we lay in bed examining a collection of naughty pictures among which was one of a woman on her hands and knees receiving the emblem of masculine virility in her bottom. Whenever Irma saw anything in pictures which struck her fancy she always wanted to put it into immediate practise. When her eyes lit on this picture, she exclaimed:

"There is something I've always had a temptation to try! And now is as good a time as ever!"

"All right, dear!" I agreed.

She slipped out of bed, got a small jar of pomade and spread some of its contents over my cock. Then, raising her night robe, and adopting the posture shown in the picture which had inspired this idea, she kneeled down, resting on her forearms. Obligingly, I knelt behind her, and placing the head of my cock against her bottom tried to insert it. I could tell from the way she flinched that the pressure hurt her. But she was determined so I continued until I had suceeded in getting the head inside. Palpably the unaccustomed distension of delicate membranes was painful to her, and though she suffered a partial intromission valiantly she made no effort to get it further in. For my part, kneeling there behind her, more interested in her reactions than in my own, I became aware of rhythmical contractions which followed each other at short intervals and which were of sufficient intensity to generate reciprocal echos in my own organism. The repeated muscular contractions about the head of my cock, quite contrary to my own inclinations, were bringing me rapidly to orgasm, and when I finally let go, Irma moaned, squirmed and gasped under the slight friction that I was unable to resist imparting during the fast few moments. When it was over and I had withdrawn my cock she insisted that though painful, the experiment had been productive of exquisite sensations.

As we lay for a while discussing the subject, I jokingly observed that if she wanted it that way she should look for a Turk, or an Arab. I heard that men of these races are formed rather different than Caucasians in that their cocks, though longer, are much more slender. In fact, this condition is referred to by writers as being one reason for their sodomitic tendencies and their inclination for boys in preference to women for sexual gratification. "Women for babies, boys for pleasure" is an axiom among these men. Due to the peculiarly slender formation of their cocks, the female organs do not provide enough constriction for maximum pleasure, and when dealing with them for purposes other than procreative, they prefer the back door to the one originally intended. It seems odd if the condition is racial as alleged, that Mother Nature did not compensate the unusual proportions of their cocks with corresponding dimensions in the cunts of their females.

To my surprise, Irma took my joking comments seriously, and waxed enthusiastic over the idea of having one of those long, slender cocks incerted in her bottom. She immediately began to speculate as to the possibility of securing an Arab for the purpose. Then another thought occurred to her and she proposed the substitution of a small boy—one whose cock had not yet attained proportions.

Supposing that the idea would be forgotten by the next day I said nor more, and soon thereafter dropped off to sleep.

But to waste no time in superflouous details, it was not forgotten and two days later when I returned to the villa after a ramble through the streets I found her engaged in bathing another street urchin, this time of masculine sex. This brazen little vagrant entirely unabashed at his nakedness, with his small cock sticking straight out under her fingering, was boasting about how many girls he had fucked.

As was her custom Irma pepped herself up for the occasion with an injection which she vainly tried to get me to share, and then, while I lolled in an easy chair in the capacity of an audience she removed her panties, twisted her kimona about her waist, and laid face down on the bed. The youngster following instructions, clambered up on top of her. His cock, after a few aimless movements between the cheeks of her bottom, was finally taken in her fingers, and started in the right direction. It went in all right without any difficulty, and up to the hilt. Irma's frantic movements her flushed cheeks her distended eyes, to say nothing of audible indications of pleasure were sufficient to indicate that the experiment, this time, was an unqualified success.

When we retired that night Irma presented me with a box of cigarettes of Chinese manufacture, and wanted me to try them immediately. I smoked two of them, one after the other, and observed a peculiar, pungent flavor, entirely different from that of any cigarettes I had ever smoked before. Even as I was speculating on their odd taste, a feeling of languidness began to steal over me. I tried to fight it off, but in a few minutes, physical sensations began to dissolve in nothingness. I did not lose consciousness; my brain and thoughts remained active, but my body seemed to have gone. I had no hands or arms or legs or in fact any corporeal body. The only physical sense which remained was that of hearing. This seemed to have become strangely acute, I could see nothing, I felt nothing but the tick of a clock on an adjacent bureau resounded like the measured blows of a hammer on a blacksmith's anvil.

Across my thoughts raced the recollection of the girl in the moving picture who had been drugged. I knew that the strange tasting cigarettes I had smoked were responsible for my condition, but it caused me no preoccupation. To the contrary I seemed to be floating in an atmosphere of superlative tranquility—a nebulous state of perfect contentment, and the sensation was delicious beyond description.

The floating drifting impression continued for some time and then gradually and peacefully, I lost consciousness.

The next thing I knew, I was awakening from a refreshing slumber, which had imbued me with rare strength, and a feeling of inexpressible vigor. My cock was standing up with a firmness and rigidity surpassing anything I had ever experienced, and felt as though it were twice normal size. I was lying on the silken covers of a luxurious couch, my limbs covered with a robe of some material so fine in texture that its contact with my naked flesh was like an exquisite caress. The sense of feeling had returned to me, and I marvelled at the softness of the bed and the beauty of the garment which was draped about my body. I lay for a while in a state of blissful lassitude then stirring myself I looked about me. The surroundings were entirely unfamiliar. Never had I gazed on such wonderous and majestic architecture nor such a medley of beautiful colors as met my vision. By what agical means had I been transported to this enchanted palace? Light was filtering in through stained glass of a hundred different hues and colors, and to my ears there came the saound of soft strange music, something like the muted strains of a mighty organ, but sweeter, richer, than anything I had ever heard before.

Suddenly I became aware of a figure standing near one of the massive pillars of alabaster, which supported the dome of this vast room. It was the figure of a little girl. She was dressed in a long gown of dark red color which, draped loosely about her fell almost to her little sandal clad feet. Her hair black as night, hung about her neck and shoulders in a cascade of soft curls. She was ravishingly, seductively beautiful.

As I gazed at her in rapt ecstasy, she smiled

and advanced slowly toward me. On she came until at last she reached the side of the couch. Still smiling, she extended her hand, and inserted it within the folds of the garment which covered my body. It went directly to my cock and closed about it. Her fingers toyed with it a moment, playing lightly over the throbbing flesh and then with a gentle clasp she commenced to work the foreskin up and down. A feeling of ineffable ecstasy permeated my being, and as its radiations intensified, I inclined my body toward her, placed an arm about her hips and drew her closer. She smiled again, and in her eyes was the understanding of age-old wisdom.

With one arm still about her hips I reached down, placing my hand on the bare flesh of her ankle, just under the edge of her robe. Inch by inch it crept upward over the soft curve of her leg, over a rounded knee, up the length of her thigh. And in the meanwhile, the play of her hand on my cock continued uninterrupted. I reached the juncture of her legs, and with blissful anticipation placed my hand over her cunt —or rather, where her cunt should have been, for instead of a warm, moist little cunt, it found a cock, small, but erect and hard! A beautiful little girl with a boy's cock!

This anomaly did not disturb me. I was in a

state in which all was perfect. If she had a boy's cock, all right. I took it between my fingers, and began to work it in reciprocation of the caress with which I was being favored. Her robe interfered with my movements and I separated the folds so that the little cock stuck out between her.

As my own organism responded to her ministrations, and the culminating moment approached, the movement of her wrist increased in velocity. The music in the distance became louder. Something white and wet flashed out of the end of the little cock between my fingers—and in the same instant my own began to pour forth its tribute. The music increased to a roar, the vast room began to whirl, and quickly all was a maze of crashing confusion. When the pandemonium died away the wonderous room had disappeared. There was no beautiful little girl, with a boy's cock and yet, dimly, vaguely, I seemed still to be clutching that warm bit of flesh.

Gradually, the realization stole over me that I had experienced a fantastic, but wierdly realistic dream. I opened my eyes and recognized the familiar surroundings. Irma was lying beside me, propped up on her elbow, watching my face intently. Her right hand was holding my cock still wet and dripping, and just beginning to wilt down. When she saw that I was awake, she broke into hysterical laughter.

"What in the world are you trying to do with my finger?" . . . she exclaimed between spasms of laughter. "You've been squeezing and pulling at it until it's nearly disjointed!"

Dazedly, I glanced downward. I was still gripping the index finger of her left hand.

"You little devil!" I answered, releasing it, "what was that stuff you gave me to smoke?"

I was really indignant and as she resented my failure to conside her act a favor, she remained silent. And to this day I have no knowledge of the exact nature of the drug which was responsible for my visit to artificial realms of magnificience and eroticism.

The parting of the ways drew near. In recognition of Irma's generosity, splendid hospitality, and the many favors she had shown me, I did everything possible to make myself agreeable to her during the remainder of my stay, and we separated the best of friends.

I passed several days wandering about the streets, or comfortably lying on my bed reading naughty French novels and magazines, collected by the score from newstands and kiosks. One afternoon as I was lazily debating the advisability of commencing preparations for my return, my detective friend presented himself. We chatted a bit and then, putting on my hat and coat, I accompanied him downstairs, intending to have a parting drink with him before saying good-bye. We seated ourselves at a table in front of a little cafe, and ordered our favorite liquors. In the process of consuming these, my companion suddenly leaned toward me and whispered:

"Glance over your left shoulder in a moment at the girl sitting at the table just behind you. I'll tell you something about her after we get away from here."

A moment later I glaced casually around. Sitting herself sipping some colored concoction through a straw was as neat a little Parisienne as I had seen during my stay in France. Apparently eighteen or nineteen yeas old, dressed in a very short skirt, her shapely legs clad in black silk hose, and wearing a blouse of white crepe-de-chene, so diaphanous that the pink, lace edged brassiere shielding her exhuberant bubbies was plainly visible, she formed a picture whose details registered themselved with lighting rapidy in one brief glance.

Not wishing to be caught staring I turned away, and a few minutes later looked around again, this time concentrating my gaze on her face. It was entirely at variance with the extreme coquetry of her apparel, and the careless elevation of her skirt, for her features were demure, modest, almost angelic in their pure beauty.

She was altogether too pretty not to awaken my instant admiration and after I had paid the account and we were of earshot I exclaimed:

"The cutest little trick I've seen since I've been here!"

My companion smiled cynically.

"Cute is right! Entirely too cute. She's a crook."

"A crook?" I repeated, incredulously.

"Yes, a crook. And a darn clever one."

It seemed incredible and I could scarcely reconcile the facts as he related them with that demure sweet face and the modest downcast eyes I had seen at the little sidewalk cafe.

"And she'd have cleaned you of every franc you possess." he answered with a dry smile.

"I'm not so sure it wouldn't be worth, at that." I added, as I recalled the multiple and diverse charms of the exquisite little houri which were visible to the eye, and mentally conjured up naked visions of others hidden beneath the silken trappings.

"Ha!" retorted my companion, "That's the funny part of it. None of the birds she snares ever gets as much as a feel of it. She's really married to this fellow she works with, and completely infatuated with him. All the suckers get for their money is to see her half naked for a few moments before the husband shows up. He's always right on time."

"How do they manage that?"

"Some system of signals probably. We'll get them sooner or later."

After I retired that night I lay awake for some time thinking of the girl. There was something about her which had touched a responsive chord in my being, and it was not to be suppressed even by the undisputable charges of my detective friend. And the more I thought about her, the stronger became my desire. I even studied the possibility of making her acquaintance and endeavoring to win her affection, but the idea was discarded with the recollection of my friend's statement to the effect that she was deeply enamoured with her accomplice. Finally just as I was dropping off to sleep, the germ of an idea came to me.

The next day I called on my friend and told him I had decided to remain in Paris a week or two longer.

"What's happened? Something new in skirts?" he asked, astutely.

"No . . . that is . . . well, I'll tell you . . : that girl we saw yesterday . . . "

"What!" he broke in, "A waste of time, son. You couldn't open her legs with five thousand francs. And it wouldn't be worth it, even if you could." he added, laughing.

"Wait a minute, now, before you start laughing. I've got a plan. It may open her legs, as you so crudely put it, without costing a single franc!"

"What is this plan?" he asked, cynically.

"Before I explain it, I want a little information."

"What do you want to know?"

"Do you know where she takes these Lotharios for their cleaning?"

"She takes them to the apartment she and her husband occupy. They move right after each operation. We know their present location."

"Do you know whether there are any other people involved, that is, have they any confederates who participate in any way?"

"No; they work by themselves. They don't need any help the way they handle it."

"You said yesterday they probably have some system of signals that enables the man to know the exact moment to come in. Do you think he is already in the building, or does he come in from the outside?"

"I can't answer that but one of the men who talked to us after deciding that he had been "framed" said that the fellow stepped into the room with an overcoat on and a traveling bag in his hand, as though he had just returned from a journey."

"Do you know where she could be found, in case I wanted to get her attention as a prospective victim?"

"At any given moment, no, but she frequents cafes, in the neighborhood we were in yesterday. But why waste your time and risk your money on a wild goose chase? Aren't there enough pretty girls on the streets of Paris without wasting time on this particular little crook?"

"I'm not interested in street chippies. See if you can't find out whether the husband secrets himself on the premises during the preliminaries or whether he comes in from outside. The practicability of the plan I have in mind depends mostly on this one detail. After you find out about it I'll explain everything.

"All right, I'll try, you're just wasting your time, son. Don't do anything foolish."

"I'll not make any move without consulting you first. If you think it imprudent I'll drop it. I'd have to have your co-operation anyway."

"Well, I'll be in to see you tomorrow evening, and let you know if I've been able to dig up anything.

I was waiting impatiently in the lobby the following evening when he arrived, and as we seat-

ed ourselves in a secluded corner, I handed him
a cigar, lit one myself, and waited expectantly.

"I've got the information you wanted, son.
The man comes in from the street. They either
have their operations nicely timed, or else a signal of some kind is passed from the window,
which by the way, fronts on the street. Their
rooms are on the third floor."

"Fine!" I exclaimed, "Exactly what I was hoping! One more question and I'll tell you my
scheme. Could you, on some pretent, arrest that
chap and have him detained temporarily?"

"I could get an order to pick him up for investigation . . . but what good would it do?" he
replied, doubtfully. "We have no kind of a case
against him, and he would be out in a short
while."

"Okay! Now I'll tell you what I have in
mind. I propose to attract her attention with a
display of money. If she rises to the bait, and
does me the honor to accept me as a prospective
victim, I'll play into her hands. Now here is
where you come in. When the appointment is
made you'll be on the job and follow us at a
discreet distance. When we enter the building
you'll wait outside, and when hubby shows up,
nab him and remove him quietly from the scene.
And I'll guarantee that if I'm assured of an hour
or two alone with this tricky Lorelei, safe from

the intrusion of wandering husbands, I'll have better success than my predecessors had. What about it? Will you help me?"

"Your idea is good in theory, but it won't work in practise!"

"Why won't it work?"

"Because she's too clever. When her man fails to show up she'll know something has happened, and find a way to get rid of you.

"She won't dare make any racket and I won't be so easy to shake. Are you willing to help me give it a try?"

"Sure! I'll help you! Make a date with her, if you can, and keep me posted. It won't cost anything to try, I guess, though it will probably knock out chances of landing the birds by frightening them off."

"What's the difference," I rejoined, "your infernal bastile is full enough already."

Before he left that evening we perfected the details of the plot.

All the next day, I loitered around the cafe where we had seen her previously, carrying with me a flamboyant roll of money, small notes on the inside, a few more pretentious ones on the outside. But my virgil was in vain. In the evening my friend called me by phone, and I was obliged to report an unsuccessful day.

"It's the neighborhood she hangs out in," he

said encouragingly, "If you keep your eyes open
you'll spot her."

It was not until mid-afternoon of the fourth
day, that my patience was rewarded when suddenly, out of nowhere apparently, appeared the
object of my search. She seated herself in-
dolently at a table in front of a small cafe, and
gave an order to the attendant.

Wih beating heart and studied nonchalance
I followed her, accommodating myself at a nearby table. With but a casual glance in her direction I ordered a bottle of vin rouge, leaned
back in my chair, and pretended to be watching
the passers-by. When I had finished the wine, I
summoned the waiter and asked for a second
bottle. And at the same time I brought forth
the "flash" roll from my pocket, peeled off one
of the larger bills, and tendered it in payment.
When he returned, I carelessly flipped a generous tip on the table, trusting that the damsel
was observing my affluence and lavishness. A
few moments later I glanced as though by accident in her direction. Our eyes met. She returned gaze for a few seconds, and then demurely
lowered her vision. I straightened up, twisted my
chair about slightly, and continued to eye her
from time to time, endeavoring to indicate with
my glances the admiration she had inspired.

For some minutes this little farce was kept up.

Finally she smiled at me—and there was an invitation in the smile.

I arose and approaching her table, begged her in my best French to permit me to join her. She consented modestly and was soon laughing delightedly at my efforts to pay her expressive compliments in French.

When we separated that afternoon, an appointment had been arranged for another meeting the following day.

For nearly a week our mid-afternoon meetings continued, and during this interval our friendship progressed rapidly. I missed no opportunities to convey an impression of prosperity and affluence, making many allusions to imaginary possessions, and business interests in England, and sighed regretfully over the fact that our acquaintance would be of short duration because of the urgency of my early return to London. And night by night, I reported the developments of the day to my companion in the conspiracy.

The sixth day she confided pensively that our visits were soon to terminate as she had just received a telegram from her husband announcing his return the following Saturday, and I knew that the moment had arived to speak my little piece. With all the passionate ardor I could summon, I exclaimed:

"Mon cherie, I just can't give you up without

something to remember you by! You know I'm returning to England next week, and if your husband is going to be here, I will probably have to leave without seeing you. Darling, don't think me bold, but couldn't we go some places and have a day or two together, all by ourselves? Some nice quiet place, where we can be alone, and spend everything of the time just loving each other?"

Chapter VII

The little hypocrite wiped an imaginary tear from her eye and assured me soulfully that she had never, never done such a thing before, and that I must think she was a light woman to have even suggested any such thing, that if it weren't for the deep affection I had inspired in her heart, she would be greatly offended, and so on.

"I know it sounds bold, darling, but I'm just crazy about you, and my only hope is that you'll be generous!" I pleaded.

"Well," she finally agreed, "I believe my husband would kill me if he ever found out but . . . I'll tell you what we can do. I'll take you to my apartment and we can spend a few hours together. It wouldn't be safe for me to go to a hotel because somebody might see me and tell my husband. You can meet me here Thursday afternoon.

That night I saw my friend, and advised him that the date for the trimming of the sucker had been definitely set and he promised to make all necessary arrangements to take care of his end of the program.

The anxiously awaited hour arrived, and punctually, in accordance with her promise, she was there waiting for me. And across the street idling before a shop window was my detective friend. She and I got into a taxi, and though I did not look behind I knew he was not very far in the background.

After a winding drive we drew up before a tall edifice, and as we got out, another car passed us slowly and came to a stop near the next corner.

We entered the building and stepped into an automatic lift. At the touch of a button the car moved silently upward and a few moments later she was conducting me down a lengthy corridor, before the last door of which she stopped, lifted a key in the lock, and we were inside.

Evidently there was no intention to delay things, for she lost no time in getting down to business. Seating herself on my lap, she pressed her lips to mine, favoring me with a voluptuous tongue caress which aroused every primordial instinct in my body, in fact so ravishingly intoxicating was the caress that for a moment I forgot, in the swirl of my emotions that it was simply calculated to render me an easy victim to a blackmailing scheme.

Her next move was to withdraw one of her

breasts from its silkenshield. Tilting it upward with her hand she pressed the nipple between my lips. To the accompaniment of expressive sighs and voluptuous shivers on her part I sucked the protuberant little tit and played my tongue over the rosy circle which surrounded it.

The movement was emotional and one of my hands, which had been resting on the bare flesh of her leg, just above the hose, began an upward exploration under the semi-transparent garment. But before it got very far, she detained me, suggesting that we retire to the bedroom where I could remove my clothing and be more comfortable.

Carrying the decanter of liqueur with her she conducted me to the privacy of the sleeping quarters of the apartment.

Placing my faith in the efficacy of my detective friend's co-operation, I slipped off my clothing, and at her invitation lay down on the bed. No sooner had I done this than she stepped to the window, and closed the Venetian shutters.

"Ah," I thought "the signal for hubby."

She returned to the side of the bed and slowly unfastened the diaphanous garment which, when removed, revealed a seductive picture. But it was not entirely a nude picture. For in addition to the silk brassiere whose form sustaining pockets fitted her pretty breasts as though molded over them, and her hose and slippers, she had on another article of apparel of old construction and which fitted like a glove about her hips and thighs. It was something like the abbreviated tights feminine exhibitional dancers use, which though effective in concealing the most intimate parts of the body leave all else exposed. Enough of this girl's body was visible to reveal a physical perfection worthy of sincere admiration and, crook or no crook, she presented as pretty a spectacle as ever delighted a masculine eye excited the envy of feminine one.

Alas, she was doomed to wait somewhat longer than she imagined at that moment, for down on the street below, a travel stained gentleman, in a dusty ulster, a small valise in his hand, returning unexpectedly from a long journey, walked right into the arms of a detective who was lounging in the doorway, and was quickly whisked into a waiting cab. He raved, swore, threatened, and pleaded in turn, but to no avail. He was not even permitted to use the telephone in the precinct station, despite his last, despairing plea.

Sufficient time had now elapsed to assure me that the gentleman's detention had been realized without a hitch, and I felt free to make a few moves of my own. My only preoccupation was that she might possibly raise a clamor which would be prejudical to my plans. But in this moment, as though the heavens themselves were in sympathy with me, or actuated by her own reference to rain, the room darkened—and preceeded by a sharp gust of wind a torrential deluge began to fall. It clattered and thundered against the sides of the building and the Venetian shutters over the windows and I knew that as long as it lasted any unusual noise in the room would be effectively cloaked from other occupants of the building.

Applying my mouth to the nipple of one of her breasts to distract her attention, I reached down and began to search for the buttoms which would release the tight garment, that up to the present had obstructed both my vision and my fingers. But I could not find them nor did I discover just where or how this singular garment was fastened. I tried to slip my hand up under it but it was skin tight and resisted my effort.

As she made no motion to assist me and comprehending that she had no intention of doing so I decided to remove it myself without wasting any more time in search of mysteriously concealed hooks or fastenings. Inserting my fingers under the waist band, I got a firm hold, and gave a quick, stout jerk. The garment ripped straight down the front.

The results were electrical. In a second's time

she was converted into a scratching, snarling, clawing little wild cat. It was all I could do to prevent her from doing me some actual physical harm before I got her clamped down in a manner which rendered her helpless.

"Cochon!" she gasped, her face livid with rage, "You've torn my panties!"

"I couldn't get them off any other way, sweetness!"

"Let me up!" she hissed.

"What do you want to get up for? Aren't we going to do something first?"

"I've changed my mind! Let me up instantly! I am afraid my husband is coming!"

"But you told me he wasn't coming until Saturday!"

"I have a presentment he's coming to-day! He may be here any minute!"

"Well, if you're afraid he may come, let's hurry up and finish before he gets here!"

Securing her two wrists firmly with one hand, I reached down with the other and pulled away the remanants of the torn panties. So closely had she kept me occupied during the brief struggle that I had not even gotten a glimpse of what the torn garment revealed—but now I glanced downward, and received a surprise.

Her cunt was as devoid of hair as that of a baby. I placed a hand on it, and found that it had been cleanly and neatly shaved within recent hours.

The discovery was interesting for I knew that when Parisian girls keep this particular portion of their anatomy shaved off it means that they are submitting their bodies to a certain caress which hair rather tends to interfere with.

In plain words, somebody is sucking them.

The contact of my hand galvanized her into fresh action and I had all I could do for several minutes to subdue her again. Finally, heaving and panting, half suffocated, she lay still. And a moment later, somewhat to my surprise, the tention of her muscles relaxed, the angry expression disappeared from her face.

"You're hurting my arms," she murmured plaintively.

Cautiously, alert for some new move, I relaxed my grip slightly

She snuggled up to me and at the same time extended her hand downward. Her fingers closed about my cock and clasped it firmly. Still suspicious of this sudden change in tactics, but seduced by the contact of her soft hand, I adjusted myself to a more comfortable position by her side and waited developments. The hand on my cock began to move back and forth, and the manipulation set a series of pleasant little thrills to darting through my body. Instinctively

I hugged her closer. The sensation was so agreeable, that for a moment I forgot her unexpected change in comportment and abandoned myself to the caress. Soon the pleasurable sensations intensified and her hand began to move more swiftly. And, in a flash, I understood what she was up to.

The little fox was attempting to jack me off, hoping to get rid of me in this fashion.

Adroitly, I slipped one of my knees between hers, and then, before she had time to realize what I was doing I had her legs apart and was on top of her, with the head of my cockright against her cunt.

"Oh!" she exclaimed, when she felt it penetrating her, "Wait! Wait! Don't do it to me that way! I'm afraid of getting a baby! Take it out! Take it out! I'll suck it instead!"

The offer was tempting, but remembering her elusiveness, I thought better not to surrender the ground already won. I gave a shove, and the result of the shove was that I found my cock sheathed in positively the tightest little cunt, not presumably virgin, of its entire career.

"Oh!" she gasped, "My husband will kill you for this!"

Curses, threats, epithets and maledictions poured from her lips in a steady torrent. Indifferent alike to threats and revilements, I

worked my cock in and out. The tight constriction was delicious, and the obscene epithets with
which she continued to shower me, instead of
dampening my ardor, seemed to stimulate it. It
was a unique experience. When the exquisite
sensations reached the maximum of their intensity I stopped moving and let the tension
relax. When the equilibrium was restored I
began again, pushing my cock in and drawing
it out with slow measured movements, calculated to prolong the pleasure as long as possible.

Meanwhile, the flow of curses and revilements
continued without interruption. But now I began
to note something incongruous. She was lifting
her bottom slightly to meet my thrusts! And
beween her revilements and the movements of
my cock as it slid in and out of the tight, little
hole, was a curious synchronism—a rhythmic
relation. It brought to my mind the recollection
of a funny story I had once heard, about a little
boy caught in the act of masturbating himself
by a maid servant who reprimanded him with a
lugubrious warning to the effect that he would
die if he did that. To which the boy, too far
along with the business in hand to stop, replied:
"I don't care if I . . .do . . . die . . . . . do
. . . die . . . do . . . die . . . do-die do-die
do-die-do-die!"

While my cock was going in, she held her

breath. And while it was coming out she gasped some epithet. But at the same time her bottom was coming up to meet each thrust.

I smiled down ino her face. She looked me angrily in the eye for a moment, and then suddenly her expression changed. She lay still for a few minutes and then, with a tremulous little "O-o-o-h!" began to raise and lower her hips with greater energy. I increased the rapidity of my own movements and at the same time released her hands which, until now, I had pinned down tightly with my own. Her arms came up and folded about my neck.

I had conquered the little vixen.

A moment later, heralded by several passionate exclamations orgasm overtook her, and as I perceived it, I let go also.

When the final tremors of our mutual orgastic exhaltation had died away, she sank limply back on the bed, one white forearm doubled across her face. The little red lips which but a short time before were hurling maledictions at me, were quiet now. In silence, I slowly desengaged myself and rising from the bed, began to put on my clothing. I was almost dressed before she stirred, then sitting up suddenly, she glanced downward, to where some starchy fluid was trickling slowly down between her thighs onto the white linen of the bed. She sprang to her feet exclaiming:

"Oh! You're probably gotten me with a baby!"

Precipitately, she rushed into the bath room from whence the sound of splashing water spoke eloquently of her precautions to avoid unwanted progeny.

I had completed my dressing when she came back into the room with a towel stuck between her legs. The spectacle she presented as she stood there eyeing me in a puzzled, undecided way, her cheeks flushed and her short black curls in disorder about her face was extremely enticing and for a moment I almost regretted having put on my clothes. Suddenly, however, I noticed tears glistening on her eye lashes. A wave of compassion swept over me, and my complacency at having bested her changed to pity. She had tried to trick me and had failed. But she was a woman. More than that—a young and beautiful one, naked and crying. What combination imaginable could be more effective to move a masculine heart?

I had intended to leave quickly for I had been in the place longer than I expected and knew my detective friend would be uneasy, not knowing just what might have transpired. But I was stirred by her melancholy demeanor. I had outwitted her, and could afford to be generous. Seating myself in a chair I said in kindly tones:

"Come here, little one. I want to talk to you a minute before I go."

Hesitatingly she approached the chair in which I was sitting. I put an arm about her naked waist and taking one of her hands in mine, said:

"You're far too sweet a little girl to be mixed up in such games as this. The police know all about it and they're just waiting to surprise you. Get out of it, honey, before they have a chance. Tell your husband to find some way to make a living without exposing you to such danger."

"Are you a policeman?" she gasped in a frightened whisper.

"No, honey, I'm not a policeman. But I have a friend who is, and he told me all about it. I knew right from the start."

To my consternation she began to weep in earnest. The tears streaked down her cheeks and fell on my hand. Touched and embarrassed, I drew her down on my lap and tried to console her.

"Now don't cry little one. There's no great harm done. There's still time to fix things up.

"Is my husband in jail?" she asked, tremulously.

"Don't worry about him. He'll be back in the morning. Maybe I can fix it so he'll be back tonight."

"Oh, will you, surely?"

'I will if I can but if I do, you must promise me' you won't let him put you in such a situation as this again."

"I promise! I promise!" she exclaimed heartfully and then as an after thought struck her, she asked timidly:

"Will he know what you . . . what . . . I mean, we did?"

"Not unless you tell him, honey. He has no way of knowing just what happened. You can tell him you sent me away when he didn't come. Heaven knows," I added, smiling, "you certainly tried hard enough!"

"Oh' you're a good man! I'm sorry I tried to fool you!"—and again she burst into tears. "The others (sob) weren't weren't (sob) like you; they were just (sob) fresh old men!"

"I expected maybe they had it coming to them all right, but they will make trouble for you sooner or later, baby," and as the tears continued to flow, I took my handkerchief and endeavored to dry her cheeks, soothing her with what reassurances I could.

Suddenly she threw her arms about my neck and began to kiss me.

"You're a good man," she repeated, and then, lowering her eyes, she whispered: "If you want me to, I'll do it with you again before you go!

Surprised and pleased, I glanced at my watch. It was getting later and every minute my stay was prolonged would increase my friend's anxiety. He might even, if I failed to appear soon, show up at the apartment. At the same time, the virginal aspect of that nude, shaven little cleft awakened powerful temptations. I placed the palm of my hand over it tentatively. Little electric-like shivers chased themselves up and down my spine at the touch, and my cock stiffened out in anticipation.

"Come on, if you want to. One more won't make any difference now, anyway."

"What do you know about psychic stimulation?" I asked, my thoughts reverting to Irma and her theories.

"Psychic stimulation?" she repeated, wonderingly, "What do you mean my psychic stimulation?"

"Oh, nothing much," I replied. "Baby, I'm British but I like France and I like some of the French customs. I have little time left, but if you're really willing, I'd like to do it to you with my tongue."

"All right!" she answered tensly, "I'd rather have it that way. I'm terribly afraid of getting a baby!" and she slipped off my knees.

Placing herself on the bed she put a pillow under her hips, separated her legs and in less time than it takes to tell, my face was down between her thighs, and my lips united with another pair of lips, which ran up and down, instead of crosswise. Two soft little hands clasped my cheeks as my tongue penetrated and explored the secret depths. And when its activities were transfered to the tiny little protuberance in the upper extremity of the naked incision, she writhed and moaned with ecstasy, and the little hands gripped my cheeks convulsively.

"Oh!" she gasped, "you're making me come again!"

The warm flesh against my mouth began to exhude moisture. Her body stiffened out, maintaining its rigidity for a moment and then relaxed.

I got up and with the towel she had cast aside, wiped off my lips.

"Before I go, tell me your name, honey. Your right name, I mean!"

She flushed at the recollection of the false name previously given me, and replied:

"Georgina."

"Georgina," I said, "if your number wasn't already drawn it would be easy to fall for you in a big way." And my words were sincere.

'It looks like I already have fallen for you." she responded pensively.

"Thank you, honey. I'll go now, and see about

your husband."

A feeling of sadness, almost of regret, that I would never see her again enveloped me as I walked rapidly down the street.

"Sentimental fool!" I said to myself, endeavoring to shake off the gloomy sentiments which had invaded my thoughts. I had gotten what I went after, but in my heart I knew I was taking something away with me which I had not calculated on, and that the memory of a litle figure, with its disordered curls and wet cheeks against my face, its breasts, firm and white pressed to my heart while I looked down over her shoulder at the softly rounded curve of a naked bottom and the lissom swell of daintily sculptured legs, glistening through the black sheen of her hose, would haunt me throughout the years to come.

Fifteen minutes later I was at a telephone, and when the call was effected, the uneasy voice of my detectice friend inquired:

"What in the world happened? I was about to take a man and go out there. Thought maybe that little witch and stuck a knife in your ribs. She stalled you off, didn't she?"

"No, she didn't stall me off. I'll tell you later."

"Well . . . I'll be . . . did you really . . . ?"

"Yes, yes; I'll tell you all about it when I see you. But that fellow . . . where is he?"

"Detained for investigation."

"Could you get him out to-night, if you wanted to?"

"To-night! Why . . . I could, I guess, but what's the rush?"

"Get him out, if you want to do me a favor. It's important to me. I've given my word, and I want to make it good. I'll get a cab and be down soon. Try and have him loose by the time I get there."

And I hung up the receiver.

The following week I was back in England.

But instead of going home, I took a room in London and in accordance with previously formulated plans, began looking around for an opportunity to invest what remained of the money grandmother had left me in some manner which would yield me a living.

After investigating many of the solicitations which came to me as the result of a small advertisement in the Daily Mail I finally decided upon revenues promised on the investment, would also provide me with employment at a nominal salary.

Once located, I applied myself diligently to the task of learning the fundamentals of the business and at the end of the first year, was made assistant manager. During this period I had dedicated my time and interest almost exclusively to the business and such amorous expansion as I permitted myself was confined to that class which is usually paid for by the hour or by the night. Fastidious tastes stood in the way of any extended relationships with the girls or women which I encountered is purely physical necessities, I remained heart whole and fancy free for something like a year and a half.

And then I met Edyth.

I found her in the unromantic, and prosaic atmosphere of a big department store—a sweet faced, modest, lovable girl of attractive personality voice, immediately set up in my heart that mysterious vibration which is a prelude to what we call love.

In the wiles and stratagems I employed and the prolonged courtship I paid her, before she finally surrendered her affections and something else to me, I shall not dwell. Suffice to say that eventually she gave up her employment, and we established ourselves in a pretty little flat in Kensington Gardens.

Of ardent and passionate nature, she unfolded like an exotic tropical blossom and enshrined with her memory are the recollections of many happy hours.

She had no vices, no eccentricities; she was just a wholesome normal, adorable girl, whose heart, starved for affection, responded with pas-

sionate ardor to my caresses, a harp which had
but waited the touch of a master to give forth
its sweetest strains.

Edyth had beenmarried, but had left her husband after a series of heart breaking disillusions.
Because of the peculiarly hard divorce laws of
Great Britain, and the unique circumstances
under which she had separated from her husband she had never attempted to secure a divorce and presumed herself to be still legally
bound to a man she nad not seen in over two
years.

The events which preceeded her separation
from this man as she related them to me were
so startling that despite the fact this biography
was intended to refer only to my own experiences,
I cannot bring myself to deprive my readers of
their telling. I shall, therefore, step out of the
picture for an interval, to transcribe the story,
exactly as Edyth, with dramatic realism, averted
eyes and frequent blushes as some of the more
succulent details were recounted, told it to me.
And, may I observe that in the telling, she employed a few words which I never previously,
or aferwards either for that matter, heard fall
from her lips.

EDYTH'S STORY

I was eighteen years old when Vernon began to pay me attentions. He was five years

older than I, and in my inexperience he seemed to me the epitome of masculine perfection. Nice looking, well groomed, gallant and attentive, he quickly captured my youthful affections. When he proposed marriage to me, my parents, solicitous for my welfare, interposed some objections for Vernon had nothing but an unimportant clerkship, and evidently had not impressed them as favorably as he had me. But this being the only tangible objection they could present against our marriage, I laughed it to scorn, and when they realized that my heart was set, they withdrew their opposition, and we were married.

I was deeply in love with my handsome husband and for a short time was ideally happy.

My first shock came when I discovered that a beautiful diamond engagement ring he had slipped on my finger, was unpaid for, and that the installments due on it were sadly in arrears. The small salary which he received had, before our marriage, sufficed for his own necessities but as he had saved nothing we were compelled to adopt methods of strictest economy. Before marriage I had been accustomed to a comfortable living, and generous parents had always provided me with money to purchase the little luxuries of dress and toilet so dear to the feminine heart. After marriage, my father con-

tinued to give me small sums destined to my
own personal use, but the pressure of domestic
obligations was such that I was obliged to use
this money for household expenses. The former
luxuries were sadly missed, but still deeply enamoured with my husband, I would not have
given him up for all the treasures of India.

But, alas, the sweetest illusions of life are
those most prone to rapid destruction.

The installments due on the ring had mounted
to a figure which in our actual state of finances
was apalling, and to save Vernon from the embarrassment of constant dunning, threats, I
silently withdrew it from my finger, and handed
it to him with request that it be returned.

This was but the beginning, and before we
had been married half a year, I began to see
life through less rosy spectacles. The sad realization that the idol of my girlish affections was
far from being all I had so confidently assumed,
was forced upon me.

Vernon was of weak character and lacked
the manly agressive qualities which women re-
quire in the men they love, and without which,
respect and admiration are impossible. Marriage,
instead of developing these latent if at all ex-
istent qualities was having just the contrary effect upon him and day by day he was becoming accustomed to lean more on me. The money

given me by my father was now accepted as a matter of course as being our main dependence in household finances, and his own salary was devoted almost entirely to personal expenditures.

I still loved Venon—but instead of loving him with respect and admiration, it was a pitying love—more as a mother might love a weak and petulant child.

When we had been married about a year, Vernon lost his position, and as the weeks went by, without a serious effort on his part to find another, I was obliged to seek employment. In this I was successful and though the pay was small between it and what my father gave me we managed to live.

Vernon spent most of the time lying around the house, smoking innumerable cigarettes and reviling his "rotten luck" as he called it. If I reproved him for his failure to make a more determined effort to improve his circumstances he became cross and irritable, and would leave the house, to return at a late hour of the night.

Now appeared upon the scene a Mr. George Tucker.

This individual came home one evening with Vernon, and was introduced to me as an old friend of my husband's. Mr. Tucker, though not of displeasing appearance, was an uncultured man several years older than Vernon, addicted to flashy clothing, and apparently well supplied with money. From the moment I saw this man I felt an instinctive dislike for him. His conversation was in bad taste, and the first evening he spent with us, he eyed me incessantly, assuring my husband that had he known what a "topping little woman" he had he would not have delayed so long in paying his respects.

After this Mr. Tucker's visits came in rapid succession. Occasionally he invited us out to cafes, cinematographic shows and cabarets, always with a vulgar, and ostentatious display of money. I would gladly have avoided his hospitality but Vernon insisted that I accompany them and reprimanded me for any display of coolness toward the man.

He assured me that Mr. Tucker was a person of wealth and influence engaged in many prosperous enterprises and that the cultivation of his friendship was bound to result in a solution of his own difficulties, and that I was therefore to treat him with the greatest consideration. I could not imagine what kind of business the man was engaged in—and doubted whether it could be anything of a very respectable nature, but when I questioned Vernon on this score, his answers were evasive—Mr. Tucker's interests were many and varied. Horse racing I found out later. Within a short space of time his visits were of nightly occurence, and when we did not go to a show or a cafe, he sat around until eleven or twelve o'clock, listening to Vernon and looking at me. My intuition coupled with the many more or less frank attentions Mr. Tucker paid me told me that he was more interested in me than in my husband. There are things which a woman instinctively knows and though I was innocent and unsuspecting to a fault I simply "felt" the things this man was thinking as he sat in our little parlor his eyes devouring my every movement, and I was astonished that Vernon did not preceive what was to me so obvious.

Soon Mr. Tucker was bringing huge boxes of candy, tied with flaming red ribbons and other gifts which, in order not to give my husband further reason to chide me for lack of cordiality I reluctantly accepted. About this time I observed that Vernon was never without spending money, which I did not doubt was being supplied by this mysterious and accommodating friend whose attention to me was likewise becoming more, and more pronounced. Vernon's slight preoccupation for the interest the man was now openly displaying in me, filled me with amazement. I could not understand it.

One night after I had shaken Mr. Tucker's

hand off my arm several times in succession, I said to him:

"Vernon, I simply can't stand that man. He is too fresh. What in the world do you see in him to have him hanging around here all the time?"

"Listen, Eedy!" replied my husband, "George is the best friend I've got and it's a damned shame you're so stand-offish with him. If you had any real interest in seeing me get on my feet, you wouldn't treat him so cold!"

"But, Vernon, what has that got to do with his having his hands on me all the time? I don't like it!"

"Aw, hell! What do you want to do? Make him sore at us?"

I subsided although I was inwardly much perturbed at my husband's singular attitude. It seemed as though each day was bringing some new disillusion.

A few nights later Mr. Tucker suggested that instead of going out for the evening we send for beer and sandwiches at his expense and enjoy ourselves at home. Vernon seconded the idea with enthusiasm and immediately volunteered to go after the necessary ingredients. Supplied with money by the always accommodating Mr. Tucker he put on his hat and coat and went out.

"Girlie," said Mr. Tucker as soon as we were

alone, "There's nothing I wouldn't do for you."

"Thank you, Mr. Tucker."

"You know, I think a lot of Vernie, but I think a lot of you, too."

"Yes, I know you are a good friend to Vernon, Mr. Tucker."

He arose, drew his chair closer to mine, placed his hand on my knee familiarly, and continued:

"I know you're kind of up against it here. A sweet little girl like you ought not to be working. What Vernie needs is somebody to back him up, and I'm the chappie that's going to do it."

He patted my knee affectionately.

"I'm sure my husband will appreciate anything you do for him."

"And you . . . ??" he whispered sentimentally, and at the same time his hand dropped down over the calf of my leg and began to squeeze it.

There was an implication in his words I didn't like. Also his act in feeling my leg in such a famliar manner aroused my anger. Moving my chair sufficiently to dislodge his hands, I said coldly:

"I am Vernon's wife, Mr. Tucker."

After a long delay Vernon returned with bottled stout, sandwiches, cheese and other comestibles.

"Well, how did you folks get along while I

was gone?" he exclaimed breezily. "You know, George,' he continued, shaking his finger with a waggish gesture, "I wouldn't trust Eeedy alone with anybody but you!"

"Damned if I didn't think you'd be safe in trusting her with pretty near anyone." responded Mr. Tucker sourly, whereupon my husband cast a sharp glance in my direction.

"You two haven't been quarreling, have you?"

"Of course we haven't been quarreling, Vernon! Mr. Tucker has been telling me how much he thinks of you."

The bottles were opened, and under the mellowing influence of the liquid contents the momentary tension relaxed and Mr. Tucker and Vrnon were soon in a good humor again. Before the evening was over I received another shock for my husband told a story which although it convulsed Mr. Tucker with laughter, suffused my face with shame at hearing it in his presence.

"Vernie, you oughtn't to tell such stories in front of Eedy! Just look how she's blushing!" Mr. Tucker exclaimed, gleefully.

As soon as he was gone, Vernon's good humor and gaiety vanished.

"What did you do to George to make him peeved while I was gone?" he asked, turning angrily to me.

"I didn't do anything to him, Vernon dear. He put his hand on my leg, underneath my dress, and I moved my chair, that was all."

"I'd like to know," he exclaimed, furiously, "why you're so damned finniky with George!"

"But, Vernon!" I protested, almost speechless with surprise, "You surely don't approve of him taking such liberties as that, do you?"

"Oh, what the hell does it amount to? He isn't going to eat you!"

I stared at him wide eyed and, changing his tones, he added coaxingly:

"Say, Eedie, why don't you loosen up a bit with George? He could do a lot for us, if you'd be more sensible. There's nothing in all this damn prudery. It isn't going to get us any place!"

As I listened to these strange words, scarcely able to believe my ears, a terrible comprehension began to dawn on me and suddenly an explanation of many things which had hitherto puzzled me made itself apparent.

I looked at him steadily, and for the first time I saw him in his true light, a weakling, a selfish, spineless man from whom the last bit of artificial gilt was gone. And in an instant every shred of affection faded away and in its place, at the recollection of all I had lost, came a cold determined longing to revenge myself.

Even as I looked at him a plan, suggested by his own words, half formulated itself in my mind.

With simulated calmness, I said softly:

"Vernon, let's get things straight. Just what is it you want me to do to help you? Do you want me to let Mr. Tucker fuck me?"

His face flushed at hearing the ugly word, but deceived by my apparent tranquility, he replied:

"Well, Eedy, George is a good scout. You could loosen up a bit with him. Of course . . ." he added virtuously, "I wouldn't want any other chap fooling with you . . . ."

"Vernon, was that why you went out tonight? You don't have to hide anything from me. Now that we understand each other, I'm going to help you but I want to know just exactly what I'm expecting to do. You've already told Mr. Tucker he could do it with me, haven't you?"

Still deceived by the suavity of my tones, he answered:

"Well . . . not exactly, but there wouldn't be any great harm if you came through to him once or twice and it would put us on easy street!"

"Very well, Vernon. That's what I wanted to know. I'll do it. But the next time you arrange it, don't go out. It isn't necessary and besides, I'm afraid of him. If you want me to let him do it with me, you must stay in the room."

"But, Eedy! That wouldn't be decent! he exclaimed, in surprise. "He wouldn't hurt you! What would he think if I was sticking around?"

"You leave that to me, Vernon. You'll have to be here, or I won't let him touch me."

"Well," he agreed, doubtfully, "we'll fix it some way."

Chapter VIII

The following day when I returned from the store I found that Vernon had prepared supper, something which was generally left for me to do and I guessed the significance of this unusual attention. But my plans were complete, and I was ready to go ahead with them.

"Seen Mr. Tucker to-day, Vernon?"

He nodded his head affirmatively, without looking at me.

"Everything fixed for to-night?"

"Why . . . ah . . . I guess George will be in, after dinner."

"All right, Vernon, dearest. As soon as we finish dinner you can go out and get some wine. Get plenty. And while you're gone I'll bathe and put on my prettiest things."

"You don't need to dress up especially for George." he said, with a shade of resentment in his voice at my cheerfulness.

"You want me to look nice, don't you?" I asked.

"Yes . . . " he answered eyeing me doubtfully, "But he's getting enough as it is, without extra trimmings!"

'Well, you get the wine, and leave the rest to me."

It was evident that my husband unexpected enthusiasm had somewhat dampened his spirits. He had supposed that my submission to this man would be in the nature of a sacrifice to necessity, an in his egotism had taken it for granted that to me it would be only a disagreeable incident. Rejoicing inwardly at his discomfiture, I looked forward with bitter pleasure to what was yet in store for him.

When he had gone I hurriedly packed a suitcase with my belongings, leaving out only such articles of apparel and toilet as would be needed that night, and pushed the suitcase out of sigh under the bed. Then, I bathed, and dressed myself in the prettiest garments of my modest wardrobe. I arranged my hair, powdered my face, and touched up my lips. My whole being seemed to have undergone a complete physical and mental evolution, and as I gazed into the face which looked back at me from the mirror, I was amazed at the transformation. I felt as though a heavy and long sustained load had suddenly been lifted from my shoulders and with its going the depressions, disappointments, deceptions of the past year had gone, too. I felt as a prisoner must feel upon release, after

weary months of confinement. A wave of exhilaration passed over me.

Vernon returned, placed the liquor in the
kitchen and stood watching me moodily. The
daintiness and coquetry of my dress was plainly
irritating to him. Though I was acceeding to
his own suggestion to prostitute myself for his
benefit, it hurt his vanity to see me making what
appeared to be an excessively elaborate preparation for the event.

"I'm half a mind to tell that guy there's nothing doing." he growled, finally.

"Oh, that would be foolish now, Vernon.
You've already promised him and besides, you've
got to have somebody help you get a start."

The sarcasm passed over his head, and he
agreed:

"Yes, I guess you're right, Eedy."

Mr. Tucker appeared promptly at nine o'clock,
and even had my husband not confessed it, I
would have guessed, from the expectant look
on the man's face that he had some reason to
anticipate a change in my attitude toward him.
His eyes fairly devoured me as they traveled
up over my legs, skirt, breasts and face.

"Sit down, George, and make yourself comfortable!" I exclaimed merrily.

"How's the little girl to-night?" he asked,
as I took his hat.

"Oh, fine George! Just in the right humor for a good time!"

The first step in carrying out the program I had formulated was to see that Mr. Tucker was provided with a generous, and continuous supply of liquor. Calling to Vernon to bring in some wine, I seated myself in a chair directly in front of the man, and immodestly crossed my legs in such a way that my rather short skirt was drawn up over my kness. I knew that some bit of naked leg above my hose must be visible to him, and as I had expected his glance immediately flashed downward and he stared as though mesmerized by the sight.

Joking, laughing hilariously at the slightest pretext, I sipped my own wine. Frequently I refilled my glass but always it was empty, thus I was not in reality consuming any great quantity and the artifice passed unobserved by Mr. Tucker, whose thoughts were evidently more occupied with my legs than with what I was drinking.

Vernon, sitting across the room from us, looked on in silence, his face reflecting surprise at my unusual conviviality. I perceived that he also was glancing surreptitiously at my legs and knew that the careless posture had attracted his attention as well as Mr. Tucker's. The difference was that while Mr. Tucker was enjoying the sight, he was not.

I tilted my chair backward against the wall, a movement which further contributed to the elevation of my skirts. Mr. Tucker was probably able to see half up my thigh. The effect upon him was instantaneous. He hastily poured himself a glass of wine, and beneath the cloth of his trouser leg an elongated swelling began to make itself apparent.

Vernon arose from his chair, came toward me, placed his hand on my shoulder and pinching it significally, said:

"Eedy, you're drinking an awful lot. Better not take any more!"

"Let the little girl enjoy herself, Vernie! The wine isn't going to hurt her!" interposed Mr. Tucker, a shade resentfully.

My plan was unfolded with admirable precision. I had counted on my husband's inherent egotism being awakened by my actions toward Mr. Tucker, and I knew that in such a state of mind he would not be very likely to enter into the festive spirit of the occasion, and would in his sullenness refrain from drinking. I wanted to keep a clear head in order to appreciate to the fullest his situation. On the other hand I intended to excite Mr. Tucker and encourage him to drink until he lost all control of himself, and under these conditions surrender my body to him in my husband's presence. I knew that to accomplish this I would have to inflame the man to the point of beastliness. Unless I could do this, he would naturally expect to consumate the act in privacy.

He was now almost drunk while Vernon had taken but a single glass, and I, by means of deft manipulation of bottles and glasses had avoided drinking much more, though I pretended to be half tipsy.

"Come on, old dear," I called to Vernon, "put a record on the gramaphone; Georgie and I want to dance!"

With reluctance, still eyeing me reproachfully, he obeyed. Seizing Mr. Tucker by the arm I pulled him from his chair. He was unsteady on his feet, but our gyrations served the purpose of enabling me to rub my leg against the place where something hard and stiff under the cloth of his trousers was throbbing and pushing.

We sat down, flushed and panting, and I poured him another drink.

"Vernon, you don't care if I sit on Georgie's lap, do you?" I pleaded coaxingly." He's a good old scout and I have to love him a little bit too, you know!"

"Go ahead, if you want to!" he responded gruffly. There was an angry glint in his eye and I felt a thrill of satisfaction. His punishment had begun.

I seated myself on Mr. Tucker's knee, and placed an arm around his neck.

"Vernon, you don't care if I give Georgie a teeny kiss, do you?"

His eyes shot fire.

"Give him a dozen, if you want to!"

I pressed my mouth to Mr. Tucker's, and inserted my tongue between his lips. I felt his body tense, and knew that every carnal instinct in the man was aroused. I touched my tongue to his, moaned, sighed, shivered, and took on as though I was in a state of passionate excitation. He placed a hand greedily over one of my breasts and I felt the fingers of the other squeezing and pinching the flesh of my thigh.

But he was not drunk enough for my purpose. I slipped from his lap, and shaking my finger in his face exclaimed with mock severity:

"Bad man. Putting his hand on Eedy's titty! Mustn't do that. Makes her have naughty feelings!"

I served another drink to Mr. Tucker. His gaze never left me as he drained it, and in his eyes I read the thoughts which filled his intoxicated brain, and knew that in imagination he was already contemplating my naked body, and mentally possessing me.

Again I sat on his knee and as if by accident permitted my hand to brush against the bulky swelling under his trouser leg.

"George! What have you got in your pocket? Why, it feels as though it was alive!"

"Ha, ha, ha!" roared Mr. Tucker, "She wants to know what I've got in my pocket, Vernie!"

My husband vouschafed no comment, but looked on in frozen silence, then suddenly arose, and walked into the dining room. It was not my intention to permit him to escape a single detail, and so, on the pretext of getting more liquor, I followed him.

"Say!" he whispered savagely, seizing me by the arm, "I've changed my mind! To hell with George! Let's get him out of here, before he gets any drunker!"

"Why, Vernon!" I replied tipsily, "Georgie's an old dear! He's the best friend we've got. I'm going to loosen up with him. Where the hell are we going to get a lot of damn prudishness?"

He tried to hold me, but I slipped from his grasp and flitted back to Mr. Tucker. Raising my dress above my knees, I essayed a half drunken dance.

"Vernon says," I declaimed solemnly, "that you're the best old scout of a friend he ever had. He says: Treat Georgie nice!"

"Sure, Vernie's my friend!" agreed Mr. Tucker thickly.

My husband returned and resumed his seat near the door.

The moment in which Mr. Tucker would be in a condition suitable to my purpose was not far off. He was now almost drunk enough to be indifferent to my husband's presence, and my familiarities with him, the exposure of my limbs, which I continually found opportunities to provide, had fired his passions almost to the limit of his endurance.

I placed another record on the gramaphone and as the disk began to revolve I piroutted about the room elevating my dress high enough to expose the bare flesh of my legs above my stockings. Mr. Tucker applauded wildly urging me on. Faster and faster I whirled until my skirt billowed outward and the short, lace edged panties I had on, were visible. I had dressed myself with just such possibilities in mind, and the panties one of my few remaining piece of finery, were of French manufacture, made of the sheerest of rose tinted silk, very short of leg, edged with narrow bands of black lace, and semi-transparent.

Mr. Tucker continued to express appreciation loudly. Stopping suddenly in front of him, I exclaimed:

"My skirt's too tight to dance in. If it wasn't for that, I'd show you some real dancing!"

"Take it off!" roared Mr. Tucker, raising instantly to the bait.

"Oooooh! That would be naughty!" I answered opening my eyes widely in shocked disapproval.

"Take it off!" cried Mr. Tucker again, his face fairly glowing with anticipation. Putting his hand in his pocket, he withdrew a five pound note and laid it on the table. "Take it off, and the money's yours!"

"Oooooh!" I repeated, 'Let you see me in my panties? Why, that's as bad almost as being naked!"

"Be a sport, Eedy!" begged Mr. Tucker, almost beside himself, and a second note was laid beside the first one.

"Well . . . " I said, doubtfully, "It's awfully naughty, but if you'll promise never, never to tell anyone . . . ?"

"Of course we won't tell!" shouted Mr. Tucker.

I took the money from the table and brazenly slipped it inside my stocking. I was going to need that money shortly, and felt that I was well entitled to it. Vernon arose from his chair, stepped into the dining room and signaled furiously to me to follow him. I pretended not to see his motions, and he remained standing in the door.

With simulated bashfulness, and encouraged on by the ecstatic Mr. Tucker, I unhooked my dress and drew it off.

He clapped his hands and shouted his appreciation drunkenly, vowing that I was the "cutest little girl" he had ever laid eyes on. With my hands on my hips, I began to weave about, as I had seen girls do in some of the vulgar shows Mr. Tucker had taken us to. My husband stood as though turned to stone till I came near him in one of my evolutions and then he whispered hoarsely:

"Eedy, you're drunk! You're making a spectacle of yourself! Put on your clothes! I'll get George away without hurting his feelings."

Heedless of his admonitions, I continued my writhings and undulations frenziedly applauded by Mr. Tucker, until breathless, I sat down on his accommodating knee. I handed him a glass of liquor which he took with trembling fingers and drained at a single gulp. He appeared to be completely oblivious to my husband's presence and probably nothing was lacking now to bring the drama to its conclusion but to permit him to follow his own drunken inclinations. He set the glass back on the table and I relaxed loosely in his arms, my hair against his cheek.

His arms tightened around me and I felt one of his hands slipping up under the brassiere which covered my breasts. It closed over one of them, and I slipped reprovingly:

"Bad, bad man! Feeling Eedy titties again and making her want to do something naughty!"

His other hand was working convulsively with the flesh of my bare thigh. Emboldened by the words, he slipped it inside my panties and for and for the first time in my life I felt the hand of a man, other than my husband, touching my sexual parts.

"Aaaah!" I breathed, shivering involuntarily.

Vernon was still leaning rigidly against the door. His face was the color of a brick and he looked as though he was suffocating.

Revenge! Revenge for my ruined girlhood, the blasting of my illusions, the months of privation!

I squeezed closer to Mr. Tucker, wriggled and squirmed as though his coarse fingering was causing me the most exquisite pleasure. Sacrificing the last instinct of modesty, subordinating the instinctive repulsion I felt for the man, I placed my hand over the bulky swelling in the front of his trousers. It responded to my touch with powerful throbs. However, limited Mr. Tucker's cultural and educational qualifications he was certainly not lacking in physical

vigor. Drunk as he was, he was entirely alive
and responsive sexually. Accommodating myself
upon his lap in such a position that every movement was visible to my husband, I unbuttoned
his pants, put my hand inside and took his thing
out. Almost involuntarily I uttered an exclamation of surprise when I saw its dimensions. Nature had endowed him generously indeed, it was
fully twice the size of my husband's and as I
had never seen any other man's but his in its
erected state, I was more than startled. Despite
the aversion I felt toward the man, the sight and
feel of it, as it jumped and throbbed in my fingers, inspired me with a strange feeling of . . .
oh, I don't know how to express it . . . a tingling, trembly sensation that went all through
me.

I recovered quickly from my momentary confusion and then, in plain sight of my stupified
husband, whose eyes were fixed glaringly upon
me, I began to fondle and toy with it. I pulled
the white foreskin down until the big, cherry
shaped head stuck out nakedly. I tickled it
with my finger-tips, squeezed it and played with
it until some big drops of limpid moisture appeared and rolled down the side. And at the
same time I shivered and moaned and pressed
my thighs together as if I wanted to do something so bad I could hardly wait.

Mr. Tucker had succeeded in unfastening my brassiere, and had uncovered my breasts. He put his mouth on one of them and while he sucked at the nipple he squeezed and massaged the other one with his hand. And at the same time his other hand was engaged in a rough manipulation of my sexual parts. He even stuck his finger up inside as far as it would go, and while I writhed and twisted on his lap he worked it in and out. I stole a surreptitious glance at my husband. He was still standing motionless, frozen.

What were his thoughts as he stood there watching another man fingering his wife's genitals while she, in an apparently half drunken but ardent frenzy, caressed and manipulated his sexual organs?

Only he could have told.

Trembling with anticipation I prepared for the final culminating gesture.

Gripping Mr. Tucker's thing firmly, I began to jiggle it violently, and exclaimed with passionate abandon:

"Oh, George! I can't wait a second longer! Quick! Fuck me!"

Jumping from his knees, I tore off my panties, and without so much as a glance toward my petrified husband, I threw myself on the floor in front of Mr. Tucker and opened my legs widely.

"Sure, I'll fuck you, girlie!" he answered thickly and without even waiting to remove his trousers, he stumbled toward me and fell upon his knees between my outstretched legs. I felt his thing punching clumsily against me and I took the thumping jerking thing in my hand and put the head in the right place. I feared that because of its size it was going to hurt me dreadfully and steeled myself for the ordeal. But Nature appears to have provided for such eventualities, imparting to the female a pecular elasticity and almost before I realized it the whole thing was insde.

I sensed an extreme tightness, my flesh was expanded to the limit of its elastical capacity, but there was no pain. And the next instant, I felt it working back and forth.

Nothing now remained, except to stage an exhibition, such as would leave no doubt in my husband's mind that I was enjoying sexual pleasure with this man greater than any I had ever experienced with him. Toward this end, I kicked up my legs, moaned, sighed, shivered, wriggled, and undulated my hips with simulated ardor, keeping up the meanwhile a series of excited exhortations and exclamations such as: "Oh, it's good! . . . Push harder, Georgie! . . . Oh, stick

it clear in! . . . Like that! . . . Oh, how delicious!
. . . Further in! . . . Clear in! . . . Harder! . . .
Harder! . . . "

My cries and exclamations excited the man
to an insane frenzy, and soon his distended
eyes and gasping breath told me that the end
was not far off. Abruptly, he slipped his hands
under my bottom, and raising me from the floor,
almost tranfixed me with the last, fulminating
thrusts of his rigid weapon.

A hot, wet stream suddenly flooded my in-
sides. It was ejected with such force that I felt
each distinct spurt as it stuck my womb. Some
of the burning stuff escaped, and ran down between my thighs.

I hadn't intended to—I didn't want to, but I
couldn't help it. I came, too. Involuntarily, I
threw my legs up and clamped them around his
body in a vise-like grip. And the last exclamations I uttered were genuine instead of faked.

When it was finished, he sank down upon
me almost crushing me with his heavy body.

I twisted out from underneath him and called
to Vernon to bring me a towel. He made no
move to obey and I repeated the command im-
periously. It was a final, artistic touch! He
hesitated a moment in dazed uncertainty, then
turned and left the room. He came back with
a towel in his hand and flung it on the floor

near me. Deliberately, before his eyes I wiped
from between my legs the exterior tracs of his
friends orgastic prowness, and tossed the towel
back to him. He hurled it aside, and with a
venomous glance at Mr. Tucker who now in a
drunken stupor, snarled:

"You damned little whore!"

I got up, and went into the bathroom where
I had already prepared, and had waiting, a
sanitary preparation.

When I came out, Mr. Tucker was still lying
on the floor, where he had fallen. He was unconscious. His pants were open, and his thing,
although wierdly diminished in size, was still
wet and dripping.

Without a word and without further pretense
of intoxication, I put on my panties, adjusted
my brassiere and replaced the waist and dress
I had removed. Going to the bedroom, I quickly
gathered up such articles of toilet as remained
unpacked and swept them into a small grip.
I put on my hat and coat, and with grip and
suitcase, left the room.

When Vernon saw me fully dressed, and with
hand luggage, his mouth fell open. For a moment he was speechless. Then he stammered:

"Why . . . where are you going, Eedy?"

"I'm leaving you, Vernon, but you'll still have
your friend Mr. Tucker to look out for you."

"But, Eedy . . . I don't . . . "

Before he had concluded the sentence the door was closed behind me and I had walked out of his life forever.

I've never seen him since and that's all there is to tell.

The dramatic effect of Edyth's story was highly intensified by the fact that she was naturally very modest, even bashful—and the scarlet flame which lit her cheeks as certain portions of the narrative obliged her to use obscene words and phrases betrayed the effort it was costing her to repeat the lurid tale.

In her sexual expansions she was the embodiment of passionate fervor. But both before, and after the act, an innate modesty cloaked her words and actions. She was easily embarrassed, and blushed furiously at anything savoring of naughtiness, and her reluctance and ingenuous confusion at being seen naked was something delicious to behold. I had seen so much boldness and had been so accustomed to having mere nudity taken quite forgranted, that her blushing bashfulness was really a delightful contrast. I entertained myself by teasing her with the deliberate intention of provoking blushes, begging her to let me see her naked or watch her while she was bathing, enticing her to take curious and unusual postures in intercourse, asking her to tell me how it felt, and how many times she had "come" etc., all of which threw her into the greatest confusion.

I have said that Edyth had no vices or eccentricities. She had however, one passionate hobby, and one pecular physical characteristic.

The physical peculiarity to which I have referred was something of a more intimate nature. She was one of those extremely rare females whom Mother Nature endows with what I not knowing the scientific term, would call a tit shaped clitoris. In my entire experience I have only encountered them in three women and one of these was a juvenile, to whom reference has already been made in chapter three of this biography.

Edyth's clitoris, under the influence of erotic stimulation, stiffened out in rigid erection, some three-eighths of an inch or more, and while so erected the slightest touch upon it was sufficient to throw her into wild frenzy. As orgasm approached, she lost all control of herself and gave such vociferous expression to her feelings as I had never listened to before. Warnings to the effect that she would surely be over-heard by occupants of adjoining apartments had no effect whatsoever. In her erotic frenzy nothing existed at the moment but she and I. Her demonstrations heightened my own excitation, but they also embarrassed me, for I knew that they could, in the stillness of the night, be heard all through the building.

Eventually, I struck on the idea of placing my hand over her mouth before she reached orgasm. The first time I did this she sputtered and chocked, and indignantly accused me of trying to strangle her, but I accustomed her to the system. She said it "spoiled" part of her pleasure, and I disliked to do it, but I didn't relish the idea of providing the neighbors with free entertainment nightly and I had observed sly smiles on their faces when we passed them in the halls.

Edyth's naive modesty and simplicity charmed and intrigued me. With the exception of the drama she had enacted for the purpose of revenging herself on her husband, her sexual experiences had been confined to the most conservative of conjugal expansions. From what she told me I gathered that her husband had not been of a very ardent disposition or else was weak sexually.

"It always took a long time for his thing to get stiff enough to go in!" she confided, with a blush.

Their sexual unions had been limited to once a week or less and it was with surprise she found that I could accommodate her every night or when so inclined, two or three times. Her disappointing married life and the period of complete abstinence which followed it, had brought her to a condition in which she was a veritable treasure house of hoarded emotions, and it was exactly at this propitious moment that I, to my good fortune, entered her life.

Her ideas as to what the proper were quaint in the extreme. Intercourse was supposed to be indulged in only at night, and under cover of darkness. To leave the light on, or in fact, to even be seen naked, was immodest. The only proper position was that in which the woman lies on her back, with the man on top. Mutual handling, or caressing of genital organs was very naughty, and as for the refinements, and perversions of love to which she had heard allusions of whose exact nature she had but vague ideas, they were not even to be discussed except in whispers.

I took a cynical and wicked delight in exploiting the innocent superstitions as fast as they came to my notice and diverted myself immensely by inciting, with my teasing and wheedling, certain conflicts between her naturally voluptuous disposition and this quaint modesty.

"Edyth, darling," I pleaded coaxingly, as prior to retiring for the night, she slipped on her night-gown before removing her under garments, "why don't you want me to see you naked? You know I love to . . . but you always have something on, just to deprive me of the pleasure!"

"Gilbert! You've seen me naked often enough!"

"Why, darling, you know I haven't seen you naked half a dozen times. You've got the prettiest form of any girl I ever saw," I would add cunningly, "I don't see why you want to keep it hidden from me."

Such a plea, of course, was irrisistible.

"Well, for heaven's sake! I suppose you'll keep on teasing until I take off my night-gown!"

And off it came, while she stood blushing before me for a moment.

"Come closer darling."

When she came within arm reach, I twined my fingers in the cluster of silky brown curls at the apex of her legs.

"I had a suspicion about what part of my form you wanted to see!"

When I learned that intercourse was supposed to be enjoyed only at night under cover of darkness I immediately developed an insatiable desire for daylight gratification.

"Edyth," I whispered one day I took her on my knees after lunch, "I want to do it so bad I just can't wait until night. Just feel this!"

"But I'm all dressed!" she exclaimed in a suffocated voice.

"All you have to do is just slip off your panties!"

A bit of coaxing, liberally interspersed with kisses, and as usual I won my point. With reddened cheeks, she unfastened the little silken garment and lay down on the sofa.

"Darling, lie face down this time. It gives me the nicest feeling to have your bottom rubbing against me!"

"Gilbert!" she protested, in shocked indignation.

In this, as always, she yielded after the requisite coaxing, turning over on her stomach.

I raised her dress, exposing the firm beautiful hemispheres, and placed myself above her with my knees between her legs. Slipping one hand down the front of her bodice over one of her breasts, I inserted the other one under her abdomen and placed my finger on her clitoris. Her bottom quivered and vibrated against my stomach, in instantaneous response to the caress.

The opportunity to let her make all the racket she wanted to was a good one, for it was midday and the noise of traffic in the street below was such to lessen the probability of being overheard. Pressing my cock into her as far as it would go, I began to titillate her clitoris with my finger. And, as I had anticipated, the show began.

"Oh! Oh! Oh! she shrieked, "Oh, that's good! It's wonderful! Oh! Gilbert, dearest, darling, Oh! Oh! Oh!"

For ten or fifteen minutes I kept her squealing and kicking, under the double provocation of a cock inside and a finger outside, and then unable to longer resist the contagious excitation my own organism released itself.

"Gilbert, did I make much noise?" she asked guiltily, after it was all over, and we had arranged our clothing.

"If there was anyone closer than Trafalgar Square who didn't hear you, I'll be surprised, darling."

"Oh!" she gasped, horrified. "Why didn't you put your hand over my mouth?"

"You know where both my hands were, dear. Tell me, honey, did it feel nice? Do you like it that way? How many times did you come?"

"Gilbert! I don't want to talk about it!"

"Why not, darling?"

"Gilbert, will you please hush up?"

The extreme sensitiveness of her clitoris and its peculiar erectile qualities set me to speculating, almost involuntarily, as to what the effect of a warm tongue onit would be. Out of respect to her, I had refrained from even tentative explorations in the way of "frenching" but chance brought up the subject one night.

We were in bed, and Edyth was lying cuddled up by me. She was in a talkative mood. She had asked me a number of questions about Paris, and my experiences there, to which I gave discreet replies, when snuggling up closer to me, she said:

"Gilbert, there's something I want to ask you about . . . " she hesitated a moment, and continued in a low voice: "A woman told me, but I don't know whether it's really true. Do those French girls really let men do it to them in the mouth? . . . And do men do it to them with their tongues, too?"

When I was able to speak with composure, I replied:

"Well, darling, the French girls haven't any exclusive patents on it! I guess women of all nationalities take it that way sometimes, if they like a man well enough. And the same thing applies to men."

"Gilbert! Did you ever do that to a woman with your tongue?"

"Who? Me? Why, no, darling," I answered, discreetly, 'I never met a woman I cared for well enough to do that. That is, until I met you. I'd do it that way for you in a minute, if you wanted it."

"Why, Gilbert! That's terrible!"

"Why is it terrible, honey?"

"It's nasty!"

"That depends on the woman. You're not nasty. Youspend half your time in the bath tub. You're as clean and sweet down there as a newly budded rose!"

"I don't mean that way! I mean, It's indecent!"

"Well, darling," I lied hypocritically, "I always thought so, too, until I met you. Someway, that sort of makes it seem different. You're so fresh and sweet I'd just as soon put my lips on this, (and I placed my hand on it) as I would on your cheek!"

She remained silent for a few moments, digesting what I had said, and I whispered insinuatingly:

"They say it feels wonderful to a woman, better than any other way. Do you want me to do it to you once that way, just to see?"

"Gilbert! Hush up!"

"Just feel how this little thing is swelling up! I'll bet it would like a nice kiss if its mama didn't object!"

Her limbs trembled convulsively and the "little thing" to which I referred was standing up and pulsing violently.

"Gilbert! . . . If you don't hush up I swear

I'll get up and sleep on the lounge! Take your hand away from there!"

"All right, darling!"

The next day, while leaving a store in which I had purchased some little gifts for her my attention was attracted to a beautiful coat on display in the window. It was an exquisite garment of genuine ermine, and a price tag announced that it was on sale at the specially reduced price of forty pounds. Business had been good and I was tempted to buy the cloak for Edyth. I turned and started back into the store but as I did so it occurred to me that perhaps it would be advisable to get her opinion on it before making the rather costly purchase.

After we had dined that night I suggested a walk. Window shopping was one of her favorite diversions and she agreed with alacrity. A bit later we were gazing into shop windows at finery temptingly displayed, and without disclosing my purpose, I steered her around, until we were in front of the store where the coat was on display.

"Look at that coat, Edyth!" I exclaimed, "Isn't it a beauty"

She gazed at it rapt eyed, and drew a deep breath.

"Oh! Isn't it lovely! And look, Gilbert, only forty pounds!"

She feasted her eyes on it, and as she reluctantly turned away, I said carefully:

"Well, honey, we'll be rich some day, and you'll have a coat like that."

It was my intention to surprise her with it the next day.

We returned to our apartment and while I sat in the library reading the evening paper, Edyth undressed, and soon I heard her splashing in the bath tub. When she finished bathing she came into the room where I was sitting with a dressing gown draped about her and sat down. She seemed to be preoccupied, and was silent until I laid down my paper. As I did so, she remarked pensively:

"I sure would like to have that coat we saw."

"Yes, the coat is a beauty. Looks like it was just made for you."

"It's a bargain, too. Only forty pounds."

"We'll be able to buy coats like that before long if business continues to improve."

"I've got ten pounds saved up now. I believe I could save the rest in three or four months."

"I'm afraid the coat will be sold long before that, honey."

I got up, and standing behind her chair, tilted her face upward, and kissed her lips. As I did so, the dressing gown fell open sufficiently to disclose a pair of luscious white bubbies, free for once, of their customary harness. And, as pretty breasts always have done, and always will, they turned my thoughts to subjects other than coats.

More with the intention of teasing her than seriously and without premeditation, I said as my hands closed over the snowy globes:

"Honey, you know we're not exactly rich, but I'll make you a proposition. Let me do that to you once, and I'll buy you the coat!"

She looked at me uncomprehendingly.

"Do what?" she asked.

"You know . . . what we were talking about last night."

She gazed at me wide eyed for a moment and then as she recollected the subject of our conversation of the previous evening and comprehended what I meant, she turned crimson and exclaimed:

"Gilbert! Stop talking about those indecent French tricks!"

"You'd look marvelous in that coat."

"Will you hush up?"

"And the price they've got it marked . . . it will be gone before noon tomorrow."

"No!"

"Just once, to see what it's like."

"No! No! No!"

And she jumped up and fled into the bed-room.

Snickering to myself, I again picked up my paper.

A few minutes later she was back again, and as I glanced at her I saw that her cheeks were still red. She appeared to have something she wished to say, and I waited expectantly.

"Gilbert . . . " she murmured, and hesitated uncertainly.

"Well, honey?"

"Gilbert . . . did you . . . really mean . . . what you said?"

"About what, darling?"

"That if I let you do that to me once, you'd buy me that coat?"

With each word the color in her face became more vivid

"Of course I mean it, honey! I wouldn't go back on my word."

There was a long silence during which her eyes were turned toward the floor.

"Well . . . all right, then!"

"Hurrah!" I exclaimed, "I've been wanting to try that so bad I just couldn't hardly wait for you to say yes!" and jumping from my chair, I lifted her up in my arms, kissed her flushed cheeks and then stood her back on the floor.

"Just this once, now, remember that!"

"Well, hurry up then and come to bed and get it over with!"

As she stood there, with cheeks blazing and eyes averted, an idea occurred to me by which additional touch of the exotic might be added to the delicious rite and without saying anything to her, I immediately began clearing off the big library table. When I had removed its divers ornaments and utilities, I told her to bring a blanket and pillow from the bedroom.

"What for?" she asked, in bewilderment.

"For you to lie on, honey. I'm going to put them on the table.

"On the table?" she gasped.

"Yes, on the table, honey. Just like a big luscious piece of strawberry shortcake. Only this shortcake won't need any cream or sugar!"

"Gilbert!" she exclaimed, in a horrified voice.

"With the coat you'll be the prettiest girl in London."

"Gilbert! I am NOT going to get up on that table!"

"Genuine ermine, too. The rest of these ladies around here will be green with envy." I continued, and without waiting for her to execute the order I went myself to the bedroom, and obained the articles referred to and arranged them neatly on the massive table.

She watched my preparations to serve her

up like a plate of after dinner dessert as though paralyzed. I could contain myself, but I managed to keep a straight face, and when all was arranged to my satisfaction, I said:

"All right, honey! Now you can take your clothes off!"

Chapter IX

Mechanically, her fingers unfastened the belt of the dressing robe and she removed the garment. Chemise, panties, hose and slippers remained. Without diverting herself on any of these, moving as one in a hypnotic trance, she slowly approached the table.

"Your panties, darling! Aren't you going to take them off? I can't do that while you have them on!"

"Well for heaven's sake! I can take them off after you turn out the light, can't I?"

"But darling, I'm not going to put out the light. I could't see to do it right in the dark!"

"Gilbert! I'm not going to get on that table naked, with the lights on! I won't do it."

"Honey, you the most persistent little "no" girl I ever met in my life. I'll tell you what we can do. I'll turn them all out, except just the mantal light."

I pressed the button which controlled the cluster of lights above the table, extinguishing them, and turned on a shaded globe on one side of the fire-place mantel. It illuminated the room with a soft, pink refulgence.

"All right, sweetheart. Now you can take off your panties and get up on the table."

"Well, turn around then, and don't look at me!"

"I can't see what difference it makes if I look!" but I turned my back obediently.

When I looked around again, the panties were off.

Under the tinted, subdued rays of light her arms and shoulders and such other portions of her fare flesh as were visible, glowed rosily, I lifted her up and set her upon the edge of the table, and with the idea of stimulating her sensibilities I filled a goblet with wine and handed it to her. She drank it and after disposing of the empty glass I gently pushed her down on her back with her knees over the edge of the table.

These preliminaries were of course affording me the most delicious thrills imaginable. In all my experience, I had never "frenched" a girl under more inciting circumstances. My cock was in a state which threatened the integrity of the buttons of my trousers, and the first thing I did after I got her stretched out on the table was to unfasten them and allow it its freedom.

I leaned over her and slipped up the silk underwaist she had pulled down over her thighs. Her limbs quivered as I raised it, and she placed an arm over her eyes. I worked the diaphanous garment upward until her breasts were completely exposed in the rosy light. With this detail complete,I drew up a chair, and placing it close to the table, sat down.

True to form, when she had lain down on the table she had clenched her legs together as tightly as she could——but I let this pass for the moment, and contented myself with caressing her legs, hips, thighs, and breasts with my hands. Then, pressing my lips to one of her legs, just above the top of her stocking and dropping kisses along the route I began an upward journey. Her limbs twitched and quivered as though each kiss were electric shock. When my lips reached the place where a dark triangle of curley hair maked the juncture of her thighs, I hitched the chair a little closer, and placing my hands on her knees, endeavored to separate them. At first they seemed disinclined to part, so I applied a little more force and gradually as I continued to urge them with a firm pressure, they began to yield.

And now, under the rose tinted light, my little sweetheart's sexual flower with its border of dark chestnut curls was revealed. I separated the moist lips, and the little tit shaped protuberance in their upper extremity, which my fingers had often caressed but my eyes never before contemplated, came into view. This was the naughty little thing which caused her to moan and squeal and go into hysterical fits whenever it was petted, and I gazed at it curiously. And even as I looked, it began to expand perceptibly in size, as though excited at merely being viewed. It stiffened out, and then shrank back slightly, repeating the process at intervals of a few seconds. I placed my fingertip upon it. It was hard and firm and pulsated vigorously to my touch.

" Are you deliberately trying to drive me crazy?" she exclaimed, in a tense indignant whisper.

"Well for heaven's sake! How much longer are you going to look?"

"Lie down, sweetheart. I won't look any more if you don't want me to!"

She lay down again, still murmuring indignant protests and an instant later my face was between her thighs. Up and down the length of the humid cleft my tongue scurried and finally settled down to work in earnest on her clitoris. It rose valiantly to meet the attack and projected itself ouward.

And then pandemonium broke loose.

Grimly, I stayed at the post—indifferent for once as to whether the neighbors might think I was slaughtering her and break in the door or call the police. Between her writhings, twisting and kicking it was all I could do to keep my tongue on the right spot. Part of the time her legs were sticking straight out on either side of me—part of the time they were flying up and down in a fantastic dance and part of the time they were clasped about my neck. She raised herself on her wrists, she dropped back and tried to elevate her bottom, she twisted and wriggled until I was obliged to seize her by the hips to hold her still. No adequate reproduction of the shrieks, moans, and exclamations with which she emphasized her frenzy is possible.

How many times she had orgasm I couldn't determine but the nectar of love was dripping within a minute or so after I had first gotten my mouth on her.

Finally, I felt her body relax. She put her hands on my head, and gasped:

"I can't stand any more, Gilbert!"

The performance had produced such a tension in my own nerves that I was not far from spontaneous ejaculation. Under the pressure of her hands on my forehead, I reluctantly yielded my position. Sliding the chair back I got up, went to the bathroom, brought a moistened towel and sponged her thighs. It was the first time I had ever performed such an intimate

service for her, but she was too exhausted to
protest.

Picking her up in my arms, I carried her to
our sleeping quarters, laid her down on the
bed and sat down on the edge by her side.

A bit later we were cuddled up in each
other's arms, in bed.

"Gilbert . . . "

"You don't have to buy me that coat. And
. . and . . . "

"And what, darling?"

"If you like to do that . . . you can do it again
. . . sometime!"

"When?"

"Oh, when you want to! Tomorrow, if you
like!"

"That's a bargain, you little old sweet thing!
Tell me honey, how did it feel?"

"Hush up!"

"But, darling, after going to all that trouble
just to find out?"

"Well, what do you want to know?"

"I just want to know whether it felt nice."

"Yes! Yes!"

"Better than the other way?"

"No . . . yes . . . oh, I don't know! Now will
you stop talking about it?"

Needless to say, she got the coat. And from
that time on I enjoyed numerous special after

dinner desserts on the big library table.

One day not long after her first surrender to cunnilingus, a matter came up, which obliged me to make a business trip to a nearby city and as the weather was pleasant it occurred to me to take her with me. It was a four hour drive by automobile so I rented a car and chauffeur for the day.

The business being satisfactorily concluded by mid-afternoon, we had dinner in a local restaurant and started back home in the evening. After an hour on the road, Edyth, who had gotten up earlier that morning than was her custom, nestled against me and went to sleep.

The position in which she had placed herself brought her cheek in close contact with a certain portion of my trousers where ordinarily a little extra allowance is made in the cloth for something besides leg. This something, always responsive to the slightest attention, and easily awakened, answered the warmth and pressure of her cheek by increasing rapidly in size. And as the pressure was not removed, it continued to expand until it reached the limit of its expansional capacity, and thereafter gave evidence of its appreciation by a series of throbs and muscular contractions.

I supposed that Edyth was now fast asleep but in this I was somewhat mistaken, for before long she stirred again. This time she raised her head slightly, her hand moved up and her fingers began unfastening the buttons on the front of my trousers. The hand slipped inside and after a bit of fumbling with interior garments came out with something warm, stiff and rigid clasped in her fingers. She adjusted the blanket so that it entirely covered her head and lay down again this time with my naked cock under her soft cheek.

I reached over and snapped out the small electric light which illuminated the interior of the car, and sat quietly with my cock throbbing between the constrictinon of her cheek and my own leg. Had she been one of the many women I had associated with previously there would not have been anything in this to surprise me, but Edyth, despite the fact that she always yielded to my coaxing, never, herself, took the lead in any of our little adventures in concupiscence. Her present action was, therefore, quite out of the ordinary.

However, I was destined for a still greater surprise.

She moved again, releasing the prisoner from beneath her face. But its freedom was only temporary, and to my amazement, I suddenly left a pair of warm lips close about it. I sat perfectly still. The lips remained motionless for a moment, and then advanced, so that a considerably larger portion of my cock was within their embrace. Another short interval of inactivity and then I perceived the pull of strong, vigorous suction and the action of a hot little tongue playing over the exposed head. So energetic and determined was the caress, that in sixty seconds or less, my testicles were threatening to release their hoarding. I placed my hand on her head to ease her away until I could again get control of the situation. But instead of surrendering the menacing thing, she pushed my hand away and sucked and still harder. And before I could avoid it, the seminal reservoirs were emptying their contents in her mouth. When I finally got free of her, I hastily handed her a handkerchief, and whispered:

"Spit it out, sweetheart!"

"I can't!" she gasped, "it went down my throat!"

"All right, all right!" I replied, hurriedly, "It won't hurt you!"

And I lifted her up in my arms and set her on my lap.

Surprises had come thick and fast, but the final one was still to come. She suddenly burst into tears and sobbed as though her heart was breaking.

"What in the world is the matter, darling?"

I asked, in utter consternation.

"Oh, Gilbert . . . I shouldn't have done that . . . you'll think I'm a bad woman now! I don't know what ever came over me!"

My sweetheart! I've done the same thing to you lots of times. Why should I think you're a bad woman?"

"You're a man. That's different. Men can do what they want to. Oh, I shouldn't have done it. Something just came over me and made me want to so bad I couldn't help it. Oh, oh, oh! Whatever will you think of me now?"

"Edyth, dearest!" I exclaimed, "Stop talking that nonsense. When a woman does that to a man, it's the greatest proof she can offer him of her affection, and if he didn't appreciate it as much, he wouldn't be worthy of her! Now stop crying right this instant!"

When I got her tranquilized she wound her arms around my neck and showered me with such passionate kisses and caused me to suspect that the favor she had done me, had provoked a reciprocal congestion in her own little ovaries, and that something was probably begging for attention.

I slipped my hand up under her dress and inside her panties. As I had divided, her genitals were dripping wet, and her clitoris standing up rigidly. She trembled as my fingers came in contact with it, placed her hand over mine, squeezed it tightly for a moment between her thighs and then gently withdrew it.

"Wait until we get home, Gilbert!" she whispered.

And the low but vibrant words augured an enjoyable termination to the adventure later.

"Are you going to let me do it to you that way, too, honey?"

Her consent for once was given without any hypocritical evasions, though she hid her face against my neck as she replied:

"Yes, if you want to!"

We reached home a little after eleven. After a bath, and some refreshments, the big table was prepared in the customary manner, the rose shaded light turned on, and stretched out voluptuously on the soft comforter while I, in pajamas, sat down in a chair between her swinging legs.

But hardly had my tongue begun to work on her clitoris than I was obliged to halt its activities because of the terrific clamor she immediately set up.

"Heavens!" I exclaimed, "You'll wake everybody in the building, honey!"

"I can't help it!" she gasped.

"Here! Hold this over your mouth!" and I handed her a towel.

Obediently she held it over her lips, and again
I sought out the little swollen tit shaped protuberance with my tongue. She gurgled and
sputtered but the multiple folds of the towel
which she pressed faithfully to her mouth toned
down the noise to less startling proportions.

After her first spend had bathed my lips and
cheeks she threw the towel aside and sat up.
Her face was as red as a peony.

"Gilbert!" she panted, "I haven't had enough,
I . . . ."

"All right, honey! just lie still a miute!" and
I pushed her back down in a reclining position.

As she lay there with her legs hanging over
the edge of the table it occurred to me that this
able might be adapted to another pleasant exercise and I stood up to make a hasty calculation. The height appeared to be about right.

"Slide further down on the table toward me,
as far as you can, honey . . . now put your knees
up . . . double them back over your stomach,
and hold them with your hands . . . that's right
. . just like that!"

The sharp angle projected her genitals outward between her thighs in the most prominent
manner and by standing there against her I
would be able to penetrate the most interior
depths. I unfastened my pajamas, casting the
meanwhile a contemplative glance at the rosy

lips projected forward. They were like a pear with a gash cut down through it from end too end, a pear cut lengthwise in two sections with little ringlets of brown hair adorning the upper extremities. I pressed closer and inserted the head of my cock between the two halves of the scarlet, pear shaped projection. A vibrant exclamation issued from the lips of the young lady to whom the pear belonged and her fingers gripped the edges of the table on either side of her. My cock slid further in, and still further until at last it was completely within the pleasant refuge and I felt soft tendrils of hair pressing against my groins. All I had to offer her was inside—all but my testicles, and these were compressed between the cheeks of her bottom.

"Now, darling," I said, recalling Irma's psychic aphrodisiacs, "I'm not going to move it for a while, and don't you try to wiggle, either. Just lie still. Don't even think about it. Put your thoughts on something else. Tell me about some of your experiences—things that happened to you before you knew me."

"Gilbert!" she exclaimed in a suffocated voice," How can I think of anything else with that thing inside me, jumping that way . . . it does, every few seconds?"

"Don't pay any attention to it! Talk about something else!"

"Well, what am I going to talk about?" she gasped.

"Tell me about your first experience."

"I never had until I was married!"

"But you knew about things before you were married?"

"Yes! The girls were always talking about it!"

"How old were you then?"

"Oh, thirteen or fourteen!"

"And knowing about it, didn't that make you curious to try it?"

"I . . . Gilbert! . . . What are you asking me such questions for?"

"Because it interests me to know, honey!"

"Well, sometimes it did!"

"Tell me about the first time, honey, your wedding night."

"What is there to tell?"

"Did it hurt?"

"Yes, a little, at first!"

"And after that . . . did it feel good?"

"Yes! But not as good as it does with you! His didn't go in as far as your does. It was lots smaller, too. It really felt better with that awful Mr. Tucker I told you about than it did with him!"

She laughed hysterically at the recollection.

"I'll swear, honey, that was the funniest thing I ever heard of. I can't figure out how you ever got up the nerve to go through with it. And the better I know you, the stranger it seems."

"I just made myself into another person that night!"

"You must have a natural genius for acting, tucked away in you. I'd like to see you undergo a metamorphsis like that myself . . . that is," I added hastily, . . . "with me, not with some other chap!"

"I don't know how much genius I have in me, but I do know there's something else tucked in methatisnearly setting me wild!"

"Honey," I coaxed, "tell me something real naughty! When two persons really love and understand each other the sharing of little intimate confidences is one of life's sweetest pleasures! I tell you every thing that occurs to me, but you keep your thoughts locked up so tight they can't even be dropped out!"

In the strained expression on her face and in her rapid breathing the effect of the erotic situation and conversation was discernible. I pressed closer to her and caressed her breasts.

"Oh!" she murmured faintly, and undulated her lips.

"Lie still, honey!" I warned.

"Gilbert! You're setting me crazy! That thing . . . !"

"Now, now!" I exclaimed, "Think about something else!"

"Gilbert . . . I . . . I'll tell you something . . . you may be shocked . . . " and she paused uncertainly.

"You can't shock me, darling!"

"Well, you know . . . what I did tonight . . . in the car . . . I've been wanting to do that so bad ever since the first time you did it to me, that I couldn't hardly keep from it!"

"Why didn't you then, darling?" I asked in some surprise.

"I was ashamed to, but I was wishing all the time you'd make me do it!"

"Make you do it?"

"Yes! I was just longing for you to grab me and make me take it in my mouth! But you never made the slightest effort," she added, resentfully, "not even when I was lying with my face right against it!"

"Great heavens!" I said to myself, "And I'm the chap who thought he knew all the wrinkles of feminine psychology!"

"Gilbert . . . I'll tell you something else . . . women like to be made to do things, not asked! . . . Then they don't have to feel ashamed afterwards . . . oh!" she added in a tense whisper, "it does feel good this way!" and she wriggled her bottom again.

"Lie still, honey!"

"Well, you tell me something now. Tell me some more about Paris!"

She listened with growing cheeks while I described several of the spectacles I had witnessed in the French capitol and though her thighs quivered frequently in response to the muscular twitchings of the cock which was engulfed to the hilt in her warm flesh, she remained fairly quiet. When I had concluded, she whispered:

"Gilbert, do you suppose there are girls here in London who do that with other women, like those French girls?"

"Plenty of them, honey."

"Gilbert . . . " she paused, and there was something in her tone which told me that another secret was going to me imparted to me. "Gilbert, I . . . it sounds dreadful, but do you know . . . " and she stopped again in confusion.

"Go on, honey."

"Well . . . I'd like to have another woman do it to me . . . just once . . . I believe . . ." and she began to giggle

"What do you believe, sweetheart?"

"Oh, nothing!"

"Come on now, what is it?"

"Well, I bet a woman can do that better than a man!"

"You little witch! That's a slam on me! Don't

you think I do it well enough? From the racket you make one wouldn't think there was any room for improvement!

"Oh, Gilbert, dearest, I really didn't mean that the way it sounded. It's just heavenly the way you do it. I mean . . . oh, I don't know how to explain just exactly what I do mean!" and there was another burst of hysterical giggles.

"You fibbed to me the other night! she added, a moment later.

"Fibbed to you?"

"Yes; fibbed to me."

"About what, honey?"

"When you said I was the first woman you ever did that to."

Not knowing whether it would be more discreet to deny, or confess my guilt, I hedged with another question.

"What makes you think I fibbed about it, darling?"

"Ha! You know too much for a novice. I realized that, after thinking about it a little. Don't think I'm so silly as to be jealous about what you did before you knew me. I don't blame you. I bet . . . " she continued, "if I were a man, I'd do it with every woman I liked!"

"How would you manage that, honey?"

"I'd make them! They're just pretending they don't want to most of the time. Men are so silly!

And you're just like all the rest of them!"

"Well, give me a few pointers, sweetheart! maybe I'll learn!"

"Asking me if you could do it to me that French way! Why didn't you just pull my legs apart and do it without asking me? I was crazy to try it, but I was ashamed to say so! You made me so darn mad! And asking me to let you see me naked—you're big enough to lift my nightgown up and look at me all you want without my helping you, aren't you?"

This discourse was delivered so seriously, and yet with expression so comical on her face that it convulsed me with laughter.

"You may be right, in part, honey," I said, when I had recovered my composure, "but sometimes there are exceptions which might make that a doubtful rule to follow. A man must be sure his attentions are welcome before he goes too far. And no man with any of the instincts of a gentleman wants to force anything on a woman against her wishes."

"Maybe you're right, sweetheart. I'll follow your advice hereafter!"

"You old darling, you've been so good to me I don't beleve I could really get mad at you if I tried."

"Happy with me, sweetheart?"

"Happier than I ever was before in my life,

even if you do tease me to do naughty things! Oh, Gilbert . . . move it a little, please, I can't be still a second longer!"

Despite my efforts to oblige her to remain quiet, she began to undulate her hips, franticly, pressing her genitals against me until, I too was caught in the current of passion. Leaning over I clasped my hand tightly over her mouth, while the turbulent waves rocked our bodies.

"What did it feel like, sweetheart?"

She sat up, looked at me for a moment, and then burst into laughter.

"It felt like somebody turned a hose on inside me! That's just what it felt like! Now is there anything else you want to know . . . or see . . . or try?"

The next day I took time to pay a visit to a certain neighborhood not entirely unfamiliar to me by reputation, which visit brought as its result an appointment with a petit little German fraulein, who was presented to me under the name of Freda. She listened attentively to my words, smiled at some of my observations, and summed up her answer in the following concise terms:

"One pound, and one extra for going out."

"We won't quarrel over the price. There'll still be another pound if you manage well."

"I'll manage it all right."

"Very well. Be ready for me to pick you up here at eight o'clock."

I telephoned to Edyth, and told her I would be a little late that evening, and would eat downtown, suggesting at the sametime that she prepare herself for a real nice "special" evening at home.

I haven't forgotten the good advice you gave me!" I added in conclusion, and heard a silvery giggle in response as I hung up.

I reached the apartment about nine o'clock and the blond fraulein was with me. Edyth looked from one to the other of us in surprise as I presented the girl, saying that she was a little friend I wanted Edyth to know. She acknowledged the introduction in a friendly way though she continued to gaze questioningly at the visitor.

Acting on the suggestion conveyed by my telephonic references to a "special" evening, she had addressed herself in coquettish dishabille not dreaming, of course, that I intended to bring anyone with me. It was evident that she was burning with curiosity regarding the German damsel, and her eyes followed me reproachfully for my failure to enlighten her regarding the mysterious visitor.

After a bit of aimless conversation I suggested that she bring in some wine, and she arose and went into the kitchen. As soon as she was out of the room, I whispered to the fraulein I would speak to her alone a moment, and followed her.

As soon as I entered the room Edyth pressed up to me and said:

"Gilbert! Who is that girl?"

"Why, you expressed a wish last night, honey, to try something and I fixed it for you."

"Gilbert . . . what on earth do you mean?"

"You said you'd like to have another woman french you once. That's what she's here for."

"Gilbert!" she exclaimed, in horrified tones. "I was just talking! I wouldn't let her do that to me! I'd die of shame!"

"Oh, yes, you will let her, sweetheart. Remember, you gave me some good advice, too. Something about "making" girls do things without asking permission first!"

"I won't let her, Gilbert! I won't even go back in the parlor while she's here!"

"Darling, you're going to let her even if I have to hold you while she does it! You run into the bedroom now, and get ready! Here . . . drink your wine first!"

She was about to voice further protests, but I interrupted:

"I mean it, honey. There's no use arguing!"

She took the glass I was profering her, drank its contents slowly and set it down.

"All right, then, if you're going to start giving

orders! I'll go in the bedroom and wait for her. But don't think you're going to watch! I couldn't, Gilbert! I just couldn't! I'd die of mortification! It will be bad enough, alone with her!"

It assuredly was no part of my plan to be absent while the experiment was in progress however, I promised her that I would stay outside promising myself at the same time that I would be far from the keyhole.

"All right! I'll go in the bedroom but don't let her come in for a few minutes," she added, blushing, "until I fix myself up!"

She threw her arms around my neck, clung to me a moment, and murmured:

"I'd rather it was you, though! I was only half in earnest when I said that. I never dreamed you'd take it seriously. But I'll go through with it now!"

"Maybe there'll be some left over for me afterwards!" I said and I ran my hand up under her dress between her legs.

She slipped down the hall, and I heard the bedroom door close behind her. I picked up the two remaining glasses, took them to the parlor, gave one to Miss Freda, and drank the other.

"What did she say?" inquired the girl, who was aware that Edyth had not at first known the purpose of her visit.

"She didn't make as much fuss as I thought she

would. She's in the bedroom waiting for you now."

"Are you coming in, too?"

"No, I said, regretfully. "She drew the line on that."

"Too bad!" said the fraulein, with a half sympathetic, half cynical smile.

She arose and I conducted her to the bedroom. She opened the door softly, stepped inside, and closed it behind her. I remained in the hall, listening attentively. At first, I heard nothing but the subdued tones of he lesbian's soft voice, answered in almost indistinguishable monosyllables by Edyth. "You're awfully bashful, aren't you, darling? . . . You don't have to be with me . . . I'm only another woman just like you . . . Oh, what perfectly beautiful bubbies . . . I'll bet your husband is just crazy about them, isn't he? . . . Why, your skin is simply marvelous! . . . As smooth and white as a baby's! . . . And no hair except where it ought to be . . . Do you know, in my country when a woman's hair down here is soft and silky instead of crisp, they say it's a sign of aristocratic blood . . . Oh, you sweet little thing! If you were mine, I'd just love you to death!"

I kneeled down to peer through the keyhole but rose again cursing under my breath. Something was draped over it from the opposite side of the door, and my vision was blocked.

Again I pressed my ear to one of the door
panels. Through it came the slight sound of
rustling garments, the creaking of bedsprings as
they ceded to the weight of moving bodies. "Wow
you lie perfectly still, darling. Let me do everything. Just relax and enjoy yourself!" Then a
silence, unbroken except for the barely audible
movement of bed-springs.

At last a faint, but expressive and long drawn
out "Ooooh!" broke the silence, followed at
short intervals by others subdued in tone yet
pregnant with emotion.

Something down in the front of my trousers
began to hitch itself upward, expanding in size
as it did so.

The exclamations continued, and became more
audible. The temptation was too much for me,
and dropping my hand down on the door nob
I turned it softly exerting a slight pressure at
the same time. The knob moved, but the door
didn't. Again I had been outwitted, for Edyth
had taken all the necessary precautions to see
that I kept my promise, regardless of whether
I changed my mind about it or not, and had
latched the door.

The music on the other side of the door, was
now beginning to run up the chromatic scale
in a way which by experience, indicated the

proximity of orgasm. It culminated in a cressendo
of vibrant moans and cries, and died away.

Another long silence and then I heard the
sound of moving feet on the floor, the murmur
of voices—words I couldn't distinguish. Quickly
I straightened up, and returned to the parlor.

A few minutes later the door opened and the
lesbian came out. She came alone. Edyth remained in the bedroom. The girl smiled, and
nodded her head as though assuring me that all
had gone well. She was evidently not disposed
to loiter, and when she had adjusted her hat
over the blond curls I handed her three five
pound notes.

"Here is my address and phone number in
case she wants me again." she whispered, and
she slipped a small card in my hand as I opened
the door.

Edyth had not reappeared, so I went into
the bedroom. A seductive vision met my eyes.
She was lying stretched out on the bed with noth-
to cover her charms except a short silk vest,
which barely reached the upper border of the
soft curls which the lesbian had called "aristocratic". The round, tapered legs were extended
out languidly, parted just sufficiently to reveal
the cleft which divided the two halves of the
altar of venus, fainly visible under the little curls
and ringlets of chestnut hair which formed its

natural curtain.

She said nothing, nor even attempted to cover her nakedness as I gazed down upon her. I was still tingling with excitement, and needed nothing more inspiring than this vision to stimulate me to quick action. I undressed as quickly as I could, and lay down by her. A second later my mouth was on her cunt, still moist from its recent spendings. She had not uttered a word and had hardly moved except to further separate her legs to better accomodate my caress, but within a few seconds after my tongue found her clitoris, the usual pandemonium was loose. I raised my head in dismay. My first thought was to make her hold a pillow over her face but even as I reached for one, a better way to quiet her occurred to me.

"Here! Put this in your mouth and let's see whether it won't choke off some of that noise!" I exclaimed, and I turned around on the bed in a direction contrary to that in which I had been lying. My cock was now projected before her face, and without hesitation her mouth opened and received it. And while her tongue curled softly around the sensitive gland, my own mouth again attached itself firmly to the humid aperture between her thighs. My tongue penetrated the most recondite depths; it played along the length of the valley and danced in circles around and over the little tit shaped protuberance which raised to meet it and then shrank back coquettishly. Almost unconsciously, my hips were moving forward and backward, and with each forward movement, my cock sank half its length into her mouth.

"Did it stop the noise?"

"Not exactly, but it did transform it from highly audible shrieks to something of a more subdued nature, a sort of gurgling, gasping, glug-glug-glug, which might possibly have been mistaken, if overheard, for the sound of water being draimed from the wash basin!"

I didn't try to delay things. As soon as I perceived that she was ready for orgasm, I let go, and as the warm essence from her ovaries baptised my face, her own lips received their spermatic recompense.

When all was finished, she pushed me to one side and leaning over the edge of the bed, spit out a mouthful.

"Part of it went down my throat again!" she gasped, comically.

A few minutes later I murmured in her ear:

"How was it that way, darling?"

"Oh, that was the best of all!" she exclaimed. fervently.

"And the girl . . . ?"

"Oh, it was wonderful!"

"Better than with me?"

"No . . . not better . . . but . . : and she began to laugh hysterically, "the way she did it was wonderful, and the way you do it is wonderful, too!" was her ambiguous answer

"Did she do it different from the way I do?"

"Yes!"

"Different in what way?" I asked, somewhat perplexed.

"Well, she . . . oh, I can't tell you!" and she went into another fit of laughter.

While I was pondering over this mystery, her demeanor became serious, and she murmured in a rather preoccupied voice:

"Gilbert . . . tell me something . . am I different in some way from other woman?"

"Sure you are darling! You're sweeter and and nicer and you have prettier titties, and legs, and arms than any other . . . ."

"Oh, Gilbert, you old exaggerator!" she interrupted, "I don't mean that way. I mean . . . down here . . . " and she motioned toward the juncture of her thighs.

"What makes you ask that, honey?"

"Well . . . that girl . . . there was something odd . . . she kept looking, and feeling . . . why, you would have thought she was a man, and I was the first woman she ever saw . . . she acted just like you did the first time you . . . kind of

. . . oh, I don't know . . . as though there was something strange about me. Maybe it was just my imagination."

I knew the answer to this of course, but fearing that, woman like, she might regard the abnormality as a defect, I changed the conversation and, still curious, endeavored to find out in what way the lesbian's caresses hand differed from my own. But my questioning only evoked more hysterical laughter and the protest that she "couldn't explain it."

Possibly the fraulein "mounted" her, but on this point neither my curiosity nor yours will probably ever be satisfied, for just exactly what the girl did to her during those mysterious fifteen minutes they were locked together, I was never able to ascertain.

Very shortly after this incident and unfortunate circumstances separated Edyth and I, temporarily as we supposed at the moment, out permanently as described by fate. She received an urgent message calling her to her mother's side. A lasting illness kept her there, and before she was free to rejoin me, I received an offer to act as commercial representative for a British firm in New York, an offer made under such advantageous conditions as made it expedient to accept.

Of my several years in that incongruous land, where "Liberty" and "Prohibition" are bedfellows, I shall tell you at some future date.

THE END